CW01081720

Other Books by Lola Keeley

Slammed
Major Surgery
The Music and the Mirror

A Roll in the Hay

LOLA KEELEY

Dedication

For Kaite, who makes it easy to keep falling
in love with a posh bird, every day

Acknowledgments

First of all to the team at Ylva – Astrid, Daniela, Alex, and the various helpers through the publishing process. You spend a lot of hours making each one of these books real, and it's a pleasure to be part of your publishing house.

I've run out of superlatives for Lee, editrix extraordinaire. This is the part where she'd leave me a comment telling me she knows I can do better and that I'll find those superlatives if I take a fresh look. Not only did she kick this book into shape, but she's been improving my writing since she first approached me to make my novels happen.

None of it would get done without the love and support of my dear lady wife, not least because she understands the process and the tricky parts. She has also finally cracked the perfect cup of tea after sixteen years, so that might be the biggest victory of all. We have a very exciting year ahead, personally and creatively, and there's no one I'd rather share it all with.

My bestie, Lande, continues to be the biggest fan and best supporter, as well as the funniest person I talk to every day. My bezzer, Lisa-Marie, provides risqué titles and podcast chats that make even book promotion fun. So many dear friends have provided comfort and support over drinks or group chats, that it would take another book to list everyone I'm grateful for. But grateful I most sincerely am.

And my parents, Isobel and Raymond, who might not entirely get the genre thing, but they'll still go to bat for me like they've been doing for most of my life. Thank you for the keeping me alive parts, that was probably a lot of hard work!

Last but never least, to every reader who has read, commented, tweeted, reviewed or emailed: THANK YOU. I hope you enjoy this book as you have the previous ones.

Chapter 1

MOVE TO THE COUNTRY, THEY said. Friendly people, beautiful animals, and rolling green fields as far as the eye can see. That was the promise in the brochures, on the websites, and in the welcoming words of everyone Tess Robinson had unveiled her grand plan to. She'd spent the past two months as a walking, talking advertisement for the excellent life choice of leaving the big city and starting fresh in the bucolic Scottish countryside. It made for the sort of heartwarming, inspirational story where Julia Roberts might play her in the film, or at least she would have done, fifteen years earlier.

Except the countryside wasn't supposed to be a dirt track with more holes in it than Swiss cheese. It cut through a field that was neither rolling nor green, but distinctly brown, and strewn with the occasional empty lager can or discarded plastic bag. The smell of manure hung on the breeze, and the only resident near the field to provide local charm was a geriatric sheep that kept bumping into the fence.

"You have reached your destination," the car's navigation system announced.

Checking her phone, Tess cursed under her breath at the predictable lack of signal. Welcome back to the countryside. As she fumbled in the glove compartment for the road map she hoped was still there, Tess couldn't help wondering if she had made a huge, life-changing mistake in leaving London. She blew the hair out of her eyes each time it got in her line of sight, which did nothing to improve her bubbling irritation.

As the icing on the cake, the rain started coming down in sheets, reducing the world to a grey, streaky mess that barely extended a few feet beyond her windscreen.

The map didn't help much at all. Her best bet would be turning around somehow and getting back to the nearest real road. Easier said than done, given the track was narrow as hell, with piled stone walls on either side. The car was practically touching them just sitting there. Turning around, even in a fifteen-point turn, seemed preferable to carrying on down the marshy field and ending up stuck in the mud. Tess decided to get the hell out of there.

She missed her zippy little Mini that she'd used to get around London—not that she'd driven much in the city. That faithful little car had been traded in when she invested in this hulking SUV that was supposed to handle every situation, but there didn't appear to be a button or a Bluetooth command for undoing bad navigation.

"Waffles, pal, I can't believe it, but I think I'm lost. And we're only about thirty miles from where I grew up." She turned around to where her gorgeous golden Labrador was staring at her from his travel crate, his usual morose expression exaggerated by his temporary confinement. "Don't worry, as soon as I find the right road, we're getting out to stretch our legs."

Knock, knock, knock.

Tess jumped at the sound. Her seatbelt dug into the side of her neck. The fist rapping on the driver's side window seemed like it was going to come through the glass. Tess saw a looming shape with a dark hood, but the rain was streaking too fast for a clear view. Her heart kickstarted a new frantic beat, but she took a deep breath and forced herself to stay calm. A glance in the rearview confirmed a proper country Land Rover had appeared behind her. She'd been so focused on Waffles, she hadn't noticed anyone approaching the car.

As she slid her window down, Tess was greeted, not with the gnarly ancient farmer she expected, but a blonde woman her own age or maybe a little older, using her Barbour wax jacket like a personal tarpaulin to keep the rain off her buoyant, blown-out curls—the sort that somehow always fall into place. Even in the middle of nowhere she looked like someone who'd just stepped out of a shampoo advert.

"I'm sorry—" Tess began.

"Never mind, sorry." Posh, then. English. Looked it as much as she sounded it. The type that would chase a teenage Tess and her friends off her land. "Can you get your impractical toy of a car out of the road? Just go forward. There's a wider part in a hundred yards where you can turn."

"Right, yeah." Tess gunned the engine before wondering when exactly this woman got the right to tell her to do anything. "You know, I really was just getting my bearings. I wouldn't have been here a minute longer, so you can just get back into your car and—"

"You're on my land, and I'd like you to not be," Blondie snapped. Some things really didn't change when it came to the landowning snobs in this part of the world. "I've already been delayed this afternoon, and I have appointments yet to attend. Urgent ones. So do move along, otherwise I'll be shunting you through one of those stone walls to make room."

Charming. Absolutely charming. Just went to show that nice clothes and pretty hair and perfect make-up didn't make a lady. Even one who could technically be described as attractive. Apart from her attitude, anyway.

No way, not happening. Tess didn't want to speculate on exactly how badly she needed to get some action if she was looking at road rage as a potential dating opportunity.

"Well?" came the impatient demand.

Waffles, bless his protective instincts, barked at the tone.

The woman glanced to the back of Tess's car. "Have you got a dog in there? Poor mutt."

"Yes, I have, as it happens," Tess says. "And he's a retired guide dog, for your information, not some mutt. Not that it would matter if he were."

Waffles added his own bellowing bark, as if proudly agreeing.

That at least got Blondie to step back from the open window, striding back to her car like the world was depending on her.

Right. Better to get on and get out of the way. Rolling down the road in second gear, Tess peered through the rain. Sure enough, there was a widening where the walls disappeared. Pulling over to the left, she waited as Lady Snooty whizzed past. Not exactly the battered farmer's model, but she'd had the cheek to judge Tess's car?

Not surprisingly, there was no wave or tooted horn in acknowledgement, just the roar of a powerful engine and the spit of gravel.

Turning back in the direction she came, Tess shook her head. Her car would be just fine, and it was far from a toy. It was about twice the height of her for a start, with more bells and whistles than she could ever possibly learn.

Edging back towards the main road, she could see where she went wrong. A rookie mistake, one that might have been avoided if she'd stuck around the area long enough to learn to drive instead of bolting for university at the first possible opportunity. Now, twenty years later, here she was, moving her whole life back, all to go into business with her best friend.

Margo was that same best friend Tess had met in their first week of university, which seemed a century ago at least. What a peculiar kind of fate that Margo, from deepest, darkest Essex, should have ended up in this wee corner of the Scottish Borders where Tess was born and raised. They were over an hour south of Edinburgh but far enough from the English border for Tess to be resolute in her Scottishness.

Heading the right way this time, she soon hit town. Well, *village* was a better word for it. The shop names had changed, and the cars parked along each side of the road were bigger, flashier, newer, but Tess recognised it. She'd come here a lot as a child, the next nearest spot of civilisation from the ramshackle farm where she'd grown up. In a movie, this would be where the soundtrack swelled in notes of joyous homecoming. For Tess's money, the banjos from *Deliverance* would have been more on the mark.

The foreboding lasted only as long as it took to park outside the vet's surgery, a sprawling cottage of a property that had been the doctor's office back in Tess's childhood. At least the rain had stopped as quickly as it started. She barely had the car door open before Margo came bundling out, still wearing her deep-green lab coat and blue latex gloves.

"There you are! We were expecting you an hour ago!" Margo collided with Tess in a hug that even rugby would deem an unfair tackle, but Tess absorbed the warmth of it with a patient smile. "Don't tell me you got lost? In your home town?"

"Okay, it's not actually my home town. And I wasn't lost!" Tess argued, but they were both already laughing. "There was an accident on the motorway, and then I made a simple wrong turn—which, by the way, would have been fixed in two seconds if some mouthy piece with a big car hadn't tried to run me off the road to get past."

"I don't think you can talk about big cars, Tess," Adam said, coming outside with a little more decorum. He'd stopped to take his lab coat off, at least.

"Oh, like you wouldn't be zipping around here in a Porsche if it could handle the roads." Tess wriggled free of Margo and gave Adam a much gentler hug that didn't risk breaking any bones. "You two look disgustingly well. And happy."

Adam and Margo beamed at each other. It was only a little nauseating. Margo wasn't much taller than Tess, who barely topped five feet. They'd always contrasted each other—Tess pale and red-headed, Margo with her dark brown bob and Italian complexion that looked tanned even when she wasn't really. Adam had that long, lean build of someone who had grown up in fresh country air, his dark hair getting a little salt and pepper. They made a handsome couple.

Only a bleep announcing some kind of next appointment reminded them that they were supposed to be doing anything else.

"Listen," Adam said, "I'd love to stay and welcome you properly, but—"

"Go," Tess urged. "I'll come help out in a minute. Just want to stretch my legs after so long in the bloody car. And Waffles must be bursting by now."

"Oh, of course he came with you!" Margo exclaimed.

Tess opened the back door and unlatched his crate. Waffles bounded out with his usual enthusiasm, a trace of pup still in him despite being fully grown.

"Well, I was hardly going to put him on the van with my furniture. That's not going to be here for ages yet. It's in storage until I get confirmation on the new place."

"I'm just glad to see him." Margo was already on the ground, giving Waffles the rough cuddles he lived for.

"You two can get back to work, I'll be fine." Tess whistled for Waffles to come to heel. He did, with obvious reluctance, and she fixed his leash, tugging on the well-worn leather of it. "Me and Boy Wonder here are going in search of caffeine and a bowl of water."

"Don't go too far, please?" Adam straightened his tie. He looked very smart for someone who spent a fair part of his week with one arm up a cow's backside. "We've got a potential new client coming in this afternoon, and she could really get our new three-way off with a bang, so to speak."

"*Partnership*." Tess sighed. "I really thought the three-way joke would have worn off by now, Adam. Is the coffee across the road any good?" She nodded to the café facing the surgery. It was past a roundabout with a delightful little garden in the middle, set around a white gazebo, of all things.

"It's kept us alive this long." Adam shrugged. "Mine's an Americano if you're buying. Now, I have a pug waiting for me."

Tess waved him off and crossed the road with the dog in tow, giving a token glance in each direction. The traffic through the village certainly hadn't increased.

The café at least belonged to the right century, with its Wi-Fi stickers in the windows and a display confirming they took cards and contactless payments. Better than Tess had hoped for, and ducking through the doors confirmed the space was light, airy, and filled with just enough comfortable chairs. The smell of freshly ground coffee competed with something sweet baking. Tess was drawn towards the counter like a cartoon character following wavy lines of deliciousness.

"Well, you must be the new vet," the statuesque black woman behind the counter said as soon as Tess stepped up. She looked to be in her early fifties. "We've been waiting for you."

"Have you?" Tess heard her own Scottish lilt deepening upon finally talking to someone whose accent matched hers. "Was the order for an Americano and two lattes in the newsletter as well?"

That got her a smile.

"Joan, by the way," Tess was informed as the coffees were being poured. "Margo said you were from around here, but I don't know your face."

"I've been away a long time. And we didn't really come here to Hayleith very much."

"You still got family here?"

"Nah." Tess shook her head. "My mum passed a few years ago, and everyone else had moved on by then. Like me, going off to Glasgow and then London, I suppose."

Joan selected lids for the coffees, taking her time fitting each one. In London that would have had Tess's impatience bursting through, but already the long drive and quiet surroundings had mellowed her just a little.

"That's a shame. Are you staying over at the vets' house? Margo and Adam certainly have the room."

"For a few days, yeah. Then I'll start settling in. Oh, I'd love to stay and chat," Tess lied through her teeth. As soon as the cups were placed in their cardboard holder, she clutched them. "It's just, you know, first day and all that. Got to show willing."

Leaving with a weak smile, she collected Waffles from where he'd been taking advantage of the water bowls by the café entrance.

They took their time sauntering back to the surgery, Waffles sniffling every inch of ground and Tess sipping at her coffee while balancing the others. Only one car passed them the whole time, and there was nobody out on the street to awkwardly say hello to. Tess caught sight of a sign for the local pub, The Spiky Thistle, just down past the vet's.

When she reached the practice's doors, a growling pug was eying its very tall owner, who was clutching a bag full of medication and bearing a grim smile of determination. That one would be back before long. Dogs refusing medicine always made for reliable repeat visitors, and sometimes at Tess's London practice it had felt like half of her actual job.

There was no one on reception, so Tess pushed through the door marked "Staff", calling out "coffee!" as she did. She stopped suddenly and stared. The chatter in the room dropped off at her shocked expression, and only one person returned it.

The blonde from the wrong road.

"As I was just saying," Margo picked up the conversation again, "our expansion is possible thanks to this lovely addition to the practice. Tess Robinson is one of my oldest friends, and we trained together at Glasgow. Tess, this is Susannah Karlson. She owns the big estate just north of here, and—"

Waffles took advantage of Tess's slack grip on the lead to promptly betray her and start snuffling around Susannah. She couldn't be entirely evil, because she paused to pet him before interrupting.

"Oh no," Susannah cut in. "Absolutely not. I didn't think you had the capacity for the Midsummer Estate anyway, but employing grown adults who can't even drive? What good will she be to me at 4a.m. in the snow when one of my horses has colic?"

"Um, actually I can drive perfectly well," Tess argued, placing the coffees on the table so her hands could settle on her hips. "Although I'm not sure a stable owner who can't handle a bout of colic alone is going to be much judge of a vet's skill."

Oops. Temper, temper. Tess had never been good with people putting her down. Anything in the region of assuming she was "less than" had historically not been great either. This woman, this *Susannah,* was a waving red rag, and Tess was absolutely the antagonised bull.

"I'm sure what Tess meant to say, Lady Karlson—" Adam began, but he seemed a little shellshocked.

"I knew this was a waste of my time. First, she makes me late for my previous meeting and now she insults my intelligence. I'm well aware of how to treat colic in my horses, but thanks for that lovely condescension. I think I'll stick to one of the big chains. An estate the size of mine needs professionals at the top of their game. Clearly this isn't where I'll find them."

With that, she swept out in a cloud of expensive perfume and gently bouncing curls.

Tess stared after her, mouth falling open. Seriously, how did women get their hair to do that? Tess had tried everything short of a perm, and still her hair lay straight and a little limp.

"Okay," Tess said, turning back to her friends. "I have no idea how that just spiralled, but I promise you, I am going to bring in new business. We don't need to be working for someone who treats us like dirt, do we?"

Adam and Margo looked at each other with that silent couple talk that concluded with a head tilt and a raised eyebrow.

"It's fine," Margo assured them both. "It was a long shot anyway; you heard her. Maybe we're not big enough for her new stud farm and whatever else she's got going on up there."

"Stud farm?" Tess groaned inwardly. The chance of working with horses had been the biggest draw about coming back to the country. That was what got her into being a vet in the first place. "I'm sorry, guys."

"Listen, we didn't have her on the books when we made our plans, so things are no different," Adam said. "I've got some neutered tomcats to wake up gently, but what do you ladies say to takeaway tonight? The house is just next door, Tess, if you want to get settled in?"

She smiled and accepted the key that Margo had thoughtfully put on a University of Glasgow keyring. Her own place, just down the road and tucked in behind the pub, wouldn't be ready for a couple of days. Tess had looked at it a few minutes ago.

"Come on, I'll show you and Waffles to the guest room," Margo said. "Then I've got a call out to check on some pigs. You can tag along, if you like, or just get unpacked."

They linked arms for the walk across to the house and, for the first time in an hour, Tess breathed all the way out. It was still going to be good, she decided. This was going to be the right move for her.

Or else.

Chapter 2

Susannah all but abandoned her Land Rover on the drive. Up until last year she'd always parked with consummate care, partly out of consideration for her late husband, who shared the driveway, and partly because of his relentless good-natured mockery of her driving skills. She stormed through the grand front doors, irked by the heft of them as they groaned their way open, but it was quicker than walking all the way around to the back. Bloody tedious, really.

The place felt too damn empty, a museum with just one living exhibit.

Spotting dust on the marble bust that dominated one corner of the room—some military-minded ancestor or other—Susannah remembered that she still had to recruit a new housekeeper. In truth, the staff had been trickling away as soon after the funeral as they could get away with, and months later, Midsummer was a stately home down to a skeleton staff. One or two quitting would have been understandable, but losing so many suggested either carelessness or a deep loyalty to her husband that didn't extend to her own management. Reflecting on that for too long didn't exactly make Susannah feel fantastic about herself.

"There you are!" Finn came hurtling towards her across the entrance hall like a security guard who had just noticed Susannah shoplifting lipstick. "I've had nothing but calls for you today."

"I'm sure you coped, and besides, I had business in the village."

"Of course I did, but what's the point in being the best executive assistant ever if you can't complain about how hard it is to be brilliant?" Looking as fashionable as ever in a dark grey shirt and skinny black tie paired perfectly with tapered trousers and low heels, Finn offered a cheeky grin.

Susannah had long since given up on trying to keep up with her PA, style-wise, just accepting the gentle criticism that was sometimes levelled at her outfits.

"Anything that can't be ignored in favour of a late lunch?" Susannah asked.

"Nope."

"Correct answer. Honestly, I've just wasted part of my day getting stuck behind some incompetent on the access road who made me late for saying goodbye to Kenny on his last day. It's bad enough I've lost him running my stables after ten years, but now he'll think I don't care one jot. Then it turns out this imbecile, who can barely find third gear, is after our vet business. I think *not*."

"Oh, the new one? Tilly, Tammy, something like that. Margo was talking to my source about her in the café last week."

Finn knew absolutely everyone in the village, but in keeping an air of drama about most things, Joan Barnes, café owner, became a *source* for the purposes of telling the story.

"Tess, actually." Susannah frowned. She had trouble remembering the names of some of her relatives most days. Why had Tess-the-terrible-driver made such an impact? Maybe it was the dog. Susannah had always had a soft spot for big, dopey Labs. "Come on, keep me company while I raid the fridge for some lunch. We really need to step up the search for a new personal chef. I'm living on what I can mine from the deli counter and whatever I can persuade Joan to stock me up with."

Having never really learned to cook beyond a burnt omelette, Susannah was missing access to a chef most of all. Even though Francine had refused to live in or work full-time and insisted on only being called *Chef* at all times, she had been a damn fine cook.

Luckily there was a platter of charcuterie and a goat's cheese salad from Joan's last delivery. There was plenty for Finn, too, so Susannah retrieved a bottle of white from the wine fridge and poured a glass for both of them.

"I assume," Susannah said, picking at some Serrano ham with her fork, "that at least half of those calls were from my dear sister-in-law?"

Finn nodded, rolling their eyes at the same time behind dark thick-rimmed glasses. "Her snivelling assistant wanted to remind you that she had sent her lawyer's letter, which I already told him you received. Then, apparently, Robin wanted to visit, even though I said you had no free time this week. And then she phoned herself 'by accident', but I think it was mostly just to irritate me. Actually I know it was, because she took the opportunity to misgender me at least three times. It's bad enough she can't use 'they' when referring to me, but the way she calls me 'girl' all the time like she's winning some kind of point…"

"Christ, I'm sorry." Susannah set her cutlery down in disgust. And maybe a little to avoid throwing anything. "You shouldn't have to put up with that level of ignorance. Not just because she has it in for me."

"Oh, to hell with Robin. It'd hurt more, all her snotty digs about both of us, if I cared about her in the least. Luckily for us, I don't. I've counted all my damns, and I don't have a single one left to spare for her."

"I wish I could be above getting irritated by her," Susannah admitted with a sigh, picking out a slice of salami. "You'd think at some point she'd realised her brother died and actually grieve for him instead of chasing his money."

"Chasing the money he left *you*," Finn corrected, since they both knew nothing else about why the will was being contested. "And trying to get control of your house and land."

"Yes. That. I know we didn't have a conventional marriage, exactly, but we did care for each other. Most importantly, we both poured our hearts and souls into preventing this place from turning into a draughty old mausoleum. Robin wouldn't be so interested if she knew how much bloody work it had taken, and how much of Jimmy's money we spent."

"She'd have a good go at spending the rest, though."

"Yes, she would. Meanwhile I have a massive estate to run, and most of the staff who left when Jimmy died haven't been replaced. As much as I don't fancy it, let's get that big vet company out to see us. They must have at least one specialist who knows horses."

"You really don't want to give the town vet a chance?"

"Didn't I just say that they're not getting my business? The first two tried to "nice me" to death, which you know I can't stand. Then the new one needs Google Maps to work out the difference between her elbow and her… well, you know."

Finn smirked, lifting their wine glass. "Thank you for being so delicate. Always such a lady, Suze."

"Lady of the manor, and don't you forget it."

"Your wicked sister-in-law certainly won't."

They both took large sips of wine in solidarity. Susannah tried not to think about all her unread emails, about the pile of paperwork in the office waiting for her signature. Right now there was just well-seasoned meat and the satisfying crunch of vegetables, along with Finn's calming company. No need to dwell on family unrest, or mouthy little vets with ponytails and altogether too much attitude.

"So the vet was really bad, huh?" Finn asked.

Susannah jumped a little at the sensation that she'd just had her mind read. "Never seen anything like it. I mean, she sounds local, so how she got lost I don't know. She was driving a tank she can't even handle, and there I find her, blocking the road like nobody else might ever want to use it. Which, fine, people take wrong turns. But she was quite content to sit there aimlessly as though the world would solve the problem for her. All thought and no action, well, that never got anything done. And like I said, it made me late for saying goodbye."

They were interrupted by the church-bell sound of the front doorbell. All that was missing were a dozen choirboys and it could have been a Sunday afternoon airing of *Songs of Praise*.

"I thought we were getting that changed," Susannah complained.

Finn got to their feet, straightening their shirt while still chewing on some rocket.

"Replacing the doorbell is on the list. It's just about three hundred places from the top."

"Oh, go answer the door."

"Fine."

Susannah had a feeling she already knew who it was, and raised voices a moment later confirmed it. She wiped her hands with the napkin and took a final mouthful of the wine. It wasn't going to end until she put in an appearance.

"Robin!" Susannah made sure her utter lack of surprise was obvious as she strode out into the entrance hall. "I didn't see your name in my calendar. And, Jonathan, here you are again, like the proverbial bad penny." She tossed Robin's assistant a withering look.

"Getting an appointment with you is nigh on impossible," Robin replied in her schoolmarmish voice, snippy as ever. She was the picture of a country wife in her sensible brogues and two layers of tweed. The streaks of grey that were apparent in Robin's hair when Susannah last saw her a few weeks before had been covered up by an aggressively auburn hair dye. And while she wore no other make-up, there was a swipe of ill-suited coral lipstick at Robin's lips.

All that was missing was the husband—but Robin, who was in her fifties, had never married. She'd somehow gotten the impression that although neither she nor Susannah could inherit Jimmy's title, the house and its land would come to her, despite the generous inheritance she'd received from their father, and the fortune she'd made investing it.

Jimmy had explained, before he met Susannah, that his money would go to some sort of charitable foundation; but the facts had never made much of an impression in this particular family feud.

"I've been trying to reach Finn here all day," Jonathan chimed in, "even on the private office line Lord Karlson gave me when I worked here. If we can't get an appointment, then what else can we do but show up?"

Robin toted Jonathan around everywhere these days like a talking handbag, and Susannah never got a better impression of him than as a sneaky little brother just bursting to tattle at the first opportunity. The fact that he dressed like the unpopular kid in a cartoon didn't help his case, right down to the fussy dark curls on his head. Well into his thirties, he had the permanent air of a man chasing his lost youth.

"Well, as you probably know from Jimmy saying it often enough, running this estate is a busy job. Not a lot of free time to chat." Susannah did her best to keep things on civil terms, but Robin's sheer entitlement drove her crazy. They'd all been born to certain advantages, but Robin was so grasping about wanting what everyone else had. Jonathan was even worse, on her behalf, and whenever he cast a glance towards a vase or a painting, Susannah had the overwhelming urge to make sure it was fixed in place.

"If you're not up to the job, there are actual *family* members more qualified. Which is why I felt I had to start this dispute in the first place. And, really, you should be referring to my late brother as Lord Karlson in front of the help. You know what they say about familiarity breeding contempt!"

"It breeds in-laws?" Susannah muttered under her breath.

"Honestly, Susannah, if you would just accept that you're in over your head, then this wouldn't need to be acrimonious. You've always been helpful. When I take over, I'm sure I could find some sort of project to keep you busy."

"Oh, could you?" Susannah advanced across the black-and-white marble floor, wishing it looked less like a dusty old chessboard. She could change that if she wanted. Maybe she could invite Robin over to watch someone taking a sledgehammer to it. "And I suppose you'd still throw me out of my house? My home?"

"Now, listen here—"

"No, I don't think I will. Finn, please show Robin and Jonathan to their car. We've got a lot to do this afternoon."

Finn did their best to corral Robin, but she was on one of her missions and wouldn't back out without getting the last word. It was funny that no matter how much Susannah looked, she could see nothing of Jimmy's kindness or quiet nobility in his sister's face. With her pursed lips and beetling eyebrows, she displayed only temper and sourness. He had always chafed at her snobbery too, how she threw around titles as if they made some people more worthy than others.

His greatest weakness, though, had been opportunistic men like Jonathan, after money and status when Jimmy had been offering simple, discreet affairs. Susannah had spent years turning the agreed blind eye as men had come and gone from the periphery, as women had quietly drifted in and out of her own life in turn.

"You'll be hearing from me. And my solicitors. You'll regret fighting me on this," Robin warned as Finn finally guided her out of the door and down the drive, Jonathan scurrying in their wake.

That left Susannah alone in the cavernous entryway, surveying the kingdom she never exactly asked for.

"Fucking hell, Jimmy. Couldn't you have broken it gently to your sister before you died? How long am I going to pay for this?"

The house held its stifling silence, of course. Susannah was getting used to the echoing emptiness with each passing day. Everything of Susannah's had come from a lot of hard work. She came from a titled family in her own right, one older and, in fact, far more distinguished than the Karlsons. Unfortunately, her father had been careless with his gambling, his drinking, and his temper, meaning their estate had all but been stripped for parts while Susannah was yanked in and out of boarding school depending on whether the fees had been paid on time.

Then, like something out of a depressing pulp novel, Susannah had gotten herself into trouble at one of the draughty old schools for sneaking vodka and kissing girls, a shame that even her usually shameless parents couldn't endure. She'd learned the hard way that her value was in snaring a husband who'd keep them all in a more reliable kind of luxury.

She'd never expected to find a kind man with secrets of his own. Jimmy had simply been looking for a business partner, a wife to keep the other ladies charmed on shoots and endless, tedious dinners. Even with money and power, Jimmy hadn't ever been able to confront where his real preferences lay.

"I need another drink," Susannah said to no one, but she ignored the kitchen and its wine. Heading upstairs to the first floor, she made a beeline for the heavy oak door, last on the right. The one thing she had achieved in this first year of widowhood was redecorating their once-shared home office, making it uniquely her own. The old décor, the wooden panels and the Oxford-library desk lamps, had been too much a reminder of her dear, departed partner. Though they'd never shared a bed, they had shared countless hours in this room plotting and planning, trying to get the best out of the estate.

Susannah stood by the fireplace a moment, the bland oil paintings replaced with splashy modern art on canvases that broke up the clean white lines of the walls as she'd redone them. The days and nights they'd worked in here, her one great frustration had been that Jimmy was reluctant to modernize. Now she had the freedom to do just that, but still the obstacles came on every side.

The office also had the benefit of a crystal decanter filled with a fine single malt, not to mention the overstuffed sofa by the huge windows, where her next stack of paperwork was crying out for attention.

"Here's to you, my old man," Susannah said after pouring a generous measure into a heavy-bottomed glass. No ice, no splash of soda. Just the unadulterated peaty taste of a twenty-year-old whisky that she'd taken a shine to. "I rather think if I'm going to piss off your sister, I'm going to go all the way with it. It's time I stopped hiding behind the details of keeping this place afloat and tried the full-steam-ahead approach."

The views out over the stunning, peaceful gardens were a balm every time she looked at them. They were all in the order of manicured lawns and geometric hedges.

Her parents had never made it to Midsummer to spoil the idyll with their entitled, drunken behaviour and pointed homophobic remarks. They'd passed in a boating accident just a few weeks before Jimmy made his proposal-cum-business-arrangement, and the prospect of a fresh start had helped Susannah through her very complicated grief. Yes, this was the place to take refuge. And the place to revive her old, ignored plans.

The first note on the pile was a reminder of her earlier appointment at the vet's. Susannah sipped her drink and snorted at the sad little sticky note. She was about to scrunch it up and toss it into the wastepaper basket, but her hand stilled before letting it fly.

Were they really so bad? Enthusiastic in the wrong ways, perhaps, but Susannah already knew how the stables would run, as a planned sanctuary for former racing and workhorses. She had the money to throw at it, but the real costs would be the veterinary care for those poor animals who'd lived a life of exertion and stress. The estate had always kept horses, but just for family riding or the odd local hunt, back in the dark days when those had still been legal.

Was it so terrible to take a chance on the plucky local vets? And even if that Tess woman was new in town today, she was almost certainly from around the area. Susannah had grown up far enough away to notice the difference. What was her story? She was not that young, close to Susannah's own forty-two years at a glance, so there must have been a life somewhere up until this point.

It was just another headache in a day full of them. The crunching of tyres on gravel signalled that Robin and Jonathan had finally gone, with their lawsuits and threats.

Susannah wished she had more people around to talk to—one of those rambling families with an aunt or a cousin just down the road. She was in the wrong part of the country for that now, even if her family could have provided the numbers. She took her phone out and skimmed the contact list. Friends left behind in Leeds, Manchester, that brief spell in London. Then the "couple friends" she'd gone out with, most often business associates of Jimmy's, who had been all right in a small-talk kind of way. No one who would appreciate a mid-afternoon rant about the difficulties of running a country estate.

Before long, she was lost in the stack of invoices and letters offering services she neither needed nor fully understood. Just another sign to push forward with her own way of doing things. If her thoughts occasionally turned to the feisty vet in a pale green sweater that hadn't hidden a single curve, well, that was just the novelty of something new disrupting sleepy countryside life.

Susannah sipped at her drink and started signing papers with a sigh.

Chapter 3

Tess was on her hands and knees on the spotless linoleum of the smallest examination room, the one that would technically be her office from now on. The dark green material of her scrubs felt familiar, like maybe her life hadn't actually changed beyond all recognition. Meanwhile, there was a six-month-old tabby kitten wedging himself under the medication locker in the corner, and his owner was already panicking that he'd escaped the table.

"Does this often, does he?" Tess asked.

"He gets into everything," the kitten's owner groaned, trying to juggle the bags she was carrying and a toddler who thought hide and seek with kitty was the funniest thing he had ever seen.

Tess suspected that Mr Giggles up in his mother's arm was probably what kitty was hiding from, far more than the vet. "Come on, little fella," Tess encouraged, wedging her hand under the cabinet and scraping her knuckles through her latex glove in the process. It was worth it when she got hold of the loose skin at the back of his neck.

In a protesting jumble of fur and skinny legs, the tabby rejoined them in the world.

Tess snuck a peek at his back end while transferring him back to the metal table to examine him. "Vaccinations today, yes? But he's getting quite mature. You'll need to book him in to get neutered."

The owner pulled a face. "My husband says we shouldn't do that to him," she explained. "Says it's cruel doing that to any man." She smiled at Tess as if she should agree and find it just as cute.

"Due respect, Mrs McDonald, it's your cat I'm after neutering, not your husband." Looking at the sticky toddler hands getting all over

Mrs McDonald's sweatshirt, Tess wondered if she should offer it as a favour anyway. It was all just a little snip and a stitch."

"Does he really need it done?"

"Only if you like your house not marked with stinky sprays every time a new smell comes into it. And you don't want your garden overrun with pregnant girl cats and their kittens."

"Oh. Well, yeah, I'd better book him in, then. I'll just tell my husband after the fact."

"Glad to hear it. These days, we give them the good drugs for it, so he'll be happy enough when he wakes up."

The chatter had let her pet the tabby into a purring state of contentment with her ungloved hand. He was a sweet little thing, even if he was called Neville, poor cat. Now it was time to quickly betray his newly won trust, and Tess reached for the needle she'd prepared before his great escape attempt.

"Right," she announced, and the injection was over before he could squirm away. "He might be a little drowsy later, so don't worry if he's slow about his food or sleeps more. He might not be in the mood to be around the kids, either."

"Oh, they never leave him alone," Mrs McDonald said. "So curious, especially at this age. He's very patient, though."

Tess resisted the urge to scoop the kitty up and adopt him. In truth, he would be fine. Plenty of family pets endured the grasping-kids phase with no problem. She just always felt a bit sorry for them, much like when she took Waffles around to her nieces, who had only just outgrown trying to ride him like a pony.

With Neville in his carrier, Tess showed the little family back to reception.

"How's it going?" Margo asked. "You're not too disappointed to start with domestic pets, are you?"

"Me? No," Tess said, although it wasn't entirely truthful. It wasn't like she expected to be wrangling pigs and sheep on day one, but part of the appeal of coming back to a country practice was getting out in the fields and dealing with challenges a little bit heftier than gerbils. "Got plenty of practice with kittens."

"Well, this next one might be more interesting." Margo nodded at Tess's tablet that displayed her next patient's details.

"Thunder?" Tess called out to the reception room. None of the waiting patients looked much like a Thunder. Then the internal doors swung open, and a Great Dane came bounding in from the patio.

Tess just managed to brace herself in time before giant paws were on her shoulders and a happy face was inches from her own.

"Down, Thunder," said a weary voice from somewhere behind, and the dog complied with a soft whine.

"Right, let's take you in here, big fella," Tess said.

With Thunder out of the way, his owner came into view. He was a short man, not much taller than Tess herself. He followed Thunder as though the dog were the one taking him for a walk, the sturdy leather leash only just keeping them connected.

Now this was a bit more like it. Tess fished out a fresh set of gloves and checked her pockets for the healthy dental treats she liked to dish out.

Adam was in the staff room when Tess slipped in for a brew, reading the *Guardian* on his tablet and half-watching the sports news muted on the decent-sized television mounted on the wall. "How's it going?" he asked, barely looking up. "Finding everything okay?"

"Oh yeah. Turns out you and Margo organise things the same way I do." Tess flicked the switch on the kettle. "Like a home away from home. Or something like that."

"How's it all coming along with your London affairs?"

Tess shrugged. "It's the usual boring whatever. Sign this, pay for that. Selling my flat was the easy part, but there's always something from the practice. Every time I think it's finalised, there's one more form, one more letter."

"That can't be much fun." Adam came over to nudge Tess aside with a gentle bump of his hip. "Margo told me how it went down with Caroline and all. She really did you dirty, and I'm sorry."

"Hey, I didn't want to share a practice with the woman who cheated on me. So trust me, this is the best outcome." Tess watched Adam pour the water into their two mugs rather than look him in the eye. She hadn't done a whole lot of talking out loud about the mess with Caroline, save for a few therapy sessions that tapered off once she made the plan to move back to Scotland. "Although the least she could have done is make the process a little smoother. I think she was hoping she could frustrate me into walking away and leaving her with everything. Some people really are that entitled."

"You think you know someone," Adam empathised.

Tess gave Adam a considering look before sighing. "Caroline was lovely…until she wasn't," was the best reply she could muster. "I've learned a valuable lesson, at least. Whatever happens, I'm keeping business and pleasure separate. We were supposed to be equal partners—in the house, in the practice—but Caroline was pulling all the strings. It's only now I've got anything that's just mine. Independent Tess from here on in. Any chance of a biscuit with this? I'm starving."

Adam checked the jar next to the kettle. "Fresh out. I'll pop across the road, get something to cheer you up."

"I'll go," Tess replied. "I saw some cakes in there yesterday that might just do the trick."

Grateful for an excuse to flee talking about her ex, Tess grabbed her leather jacket from the coat rack and slipped out.

The café was much busier today, full of people looking for a mid-morning caffeine fix and, by the sounds of it, a dose of the local gossip. The low burr of shared conversations came to a sudden halt as Tess walked in, but she gave a vague sort of tight smile until everyone went back to pretending they hadn't stopped and stared.

"Two slices of carrot cake, please, Joan." Tess aimed for friendly. "Sorry I had to dash yesterday. Can I get a cuppa with that too?" Her tea would be going cold back at the surgery, but she was in no rush to return for more pitying looks from Adam, and her next patient wasn't for twenty minutes.

"What kind?" Joan gestured to the selection of teas behind her. "Or did you mean real tea? Hard to tell with you big-city types."

"London didn't spoil my appreciation for a proper cup of tea," Tess replied. "Never really went in for that herbal stuff."

If it was a test, Joan's nod suggested Tess had passed. It reminded her of her own mum, whose constant worry until she passed away five years ago was that Tess would have her head turned by too many urban and sophisticated things. Every phone call had featured at least five minutes of fretting that Tess was losing her natural accent or forgetting where she came from. Maybe if she had actually done those things, Caroline would have found her more suitable as a long-term prospect.

"Settling in okay?" Joan fetched the carrot cake from the glass display unit between them. She sliced it up with steady hands and a very big knife.

"Yeah, it's great so far. Was a bit tired from all the driving, but I feel much better today. I'll have to explore the village a bit. Haven't even been to the pub yet, just raided Margo's wine rack last night. Although what kind of name is The Spiky Thistle, anyway?"

Joan gave a haughty little sniff. She boxed up the cake and tied it with a strip of ribbon before Tess could say all the presentation wasn't necessary. "You might want to look farther afield if you're the drinking type." A small gold cross glinted against the dark skin at Joan's throat, the light wrinkles there the only outward sign she was middle-aged. Tess felt a familiar sinking sort of panic. She'd never had great luck with organised religion, and even less so in small towns like Hayleith.

"Oh, I'm not judging, silly girl." Joan said, picking up on the way Tess had tensed. "I just don't care for what we call a drinking establishment around here. I much prefer the Kilted Coo, two towns over. But a lot of people just drink at home of an evening. Unless there's something on."

Relaxing again, Tess accepted her boxed cake and waited for her tea. When the rest of her stuff arrived, she would have to dig out a travel mug or two. All these cardboard cups were a waste, and she had enough worries as it was without feeling responsible for polluting the whole planet. "I'm sure I'll check it out," she answered as the milk was poured in without her having to ask. The strong but milky tea was exactly how she liked it. "Can't be going to the same place all the time."

"Good." There was clearly more to Joan's dislike of the pub, but Tess knew better than to ask.

She had the strongest memory all of a sudden, of being tiny, in her school uniform with a puffy anorak over it, waiting in place after place as her mum exchanged life stories with perfect strangers. Those strange pangs of missing her had gotten less frequent in the past five years, but it still felt disloyal to remember that impatience of a little kid who just wanted to get home instead of listening to boring grown-ups.

"Thanks for this," Tess added as she tapped her credit card on the reader. The cake box and cup carrier were in her hands a moment later. "You don't do loyalty cards, do you?"

Joan's glare could have reduced a lesser woman to stone, but Tess held her head high.

"I just like collecting the little stamps, that's all. Maybe you can consider it."

"I've been running this place for ten years. I know what people like," Joan said. "And I ran the pub for long enough before that. I know what I'm doing, but thank you, Dr Robinson."

"I wasn't trying to—"

"I know! You're fine, girl." Joan shooed her away, her lime green nails contrasting beautifully with the dark skin of her hands. "Give Margo and Adam my love. Tell her I got in that coffee that she likes."

"Will do," Tess says, relieved to be escaping. "Maybe I'll see you in that Kilted Coo sometime?"

"Maybe you will. Maybe you will."

Chapter 4

Susannah shoved the magazine she'd been flipping through into the smart leather laptop bag that went with her outfit and stepped off the train onto the platform at Edinburgh Waverley. Even on a sunny day, it was a cold and draughty building, the high glass ceilings pretty but not very effective. All around her, the last swarm of morning commuters raced each other to the ticket gates, but she kept her pace to a stroll, the click of her heels echoing as she made her way towards the escalators.

Usually she would have driven up to the city, but meeting at the Balmoral Hotel made the train more practical.

She was dressed to kill for this meeting, the one that could make all her plans for Midsummer Estate come true. Checking her reflection in the shop windows as she rode the escalator up, the crisp, white blouse and soft, grey trouser suit looked every bit as good as it had before leaving the house. Both hair and make-up were pretty much flawless, which was exactly what she had hoped for.

It was important she be there first, sitting at the table and sipping a coffee like she had all the time in the world. She only pretended to hate those business psychology books sold in airports. In truth, she'd picked up more than a few tips from them.

The doorman in his kilt and formal jacket nodded before opening the heavy oak door for her. Inside, the reception was a huge, refreshing sea of creamy white, populated only by a few staff and a gaggle of tourists in golf gear surrounded by their cases. The sight of the golf bags and clubs, all covered in a variety of those woollen sock things, brought back the thought of Jimmy so clearly, he might be standing next to her. It was so vivid that Susannah actually glanced over her shoulder to be sure he wasn't there.

"Lady Karlson?" The concierge, in his smart suit, greeted her like an old friend. "Mr Greer is waiting for you in Palm Court."

So much for getting ahead of the game. She followed, heels clicking on the marble floor until it gave way to plush carpet. The tea room was something out of a colonial wet dream, but at least it was familiar ground. The place was all but deserted since it was normally set aside just for afternoon tea. Mr Greer was a wealthy American, though, and for him, most hotels would make any exception.

A short, balding man, he stood to greet her, and Susannah resisted the urge to slump her shoulders and shrink by an inch or two. Instead she took her offered seat quickly and ordered "a proper cup of tea," which made the waiter roll his eyes a little but drew a smile from Mr Greer. Anglophiles were always easily pleased by little British quirks like that.

"It's a pleasure to see you, Lady Karlson. I was so sorry to hear about your husband. Lord Karlson was a fine, fine man. And, I hope I can say, a dear friend."

For a moment, she worried there was an implication to that. Then she remembered that Mr Greer had a wife back in Cape Cod, or wherever his huge mansion was, and heaved a quiet sigh of relief. Jimmy had always been meticulous about never mixing business and pleasure. He'd been the soul of discretion the whole time they were married.

"Thank you. He valued your friendship very much, Mr Greer. It's been a difficult time, but I'm muddling through as best I can. Which is part of why I requested this meeting. I know you said last year that you'd be very interested in our plans for Midsummer, and I've drawn up a proposal that shows just how ambitious and exciting it's going to be."

Their tea was served then, by a bright-eyed redhead in a sensible skirt and flat shoes. She surveyed them both before responding to Susannah's discreet once-over glance with a shy smile. That little result was as much as Susannah could risk during a business meeting. Her own sanctioned affairs had always been painfully discreet too.

"Lord Karlson always said you were pushing him to modernize the place." Mr Greer peered at her over his wire-framed glasses, his eyes watery behind them. "He liked it just as it was. But you have plans to change it all by yourself?"

"Don't see that I have much choice." Susannah kept her voice level. This was the doubt she had expected, but it made her grit her teeth all the same. "Of course, you and Lord Karlson worked together for years. You saw how involved I've been with the business. It was his wish that I carry on his legacy. That means letting Midsummer Estate evolve."

"Oh yes, yes, of course."

"I've been running it single-handedly for almost a year now. I have a great team in place, and I really think there's more potential to tap. Very lucrative potential, Mr Greer. Jim always said that nobody understood potential better than you."

He preened at the compliment, just as she'd hoped.

"Well, I do have a certain eye for a good investment," he replied, leaning back in his chair just a little. "Do tell me more, Lady Karlson."

"Only if you call me Susannah."

"Very well, Susannah. Wow me with your plans for Midsummer."

She set her teacup back in its dainty china saucer and reached for her bag. Pulling out the tablet, she took a deep breath and pitched her damn heart out.

On the drive home from the station, Susannah blasted a playlist that Finn had made for her, jokingly titled "Kicking Ass and Taking Names". It was full of the early nineties songs she'd loved as a teenager, ones she didn't realise she still knew the lyrics to. Yet, every time the drums started a new beat and the guitars came in heavy, Susannah was right there with the words on the tip of her tongue.

Five minutes from home, she got a text that she really should have pulled over to read, but she gave it a quick skim anyway. She was needed in the village.

Great. Just when her day had been going so well. She wrangled the Land Rover in the opposite direction, turning the music down to concentrate better.

Parking behind the pub in the staff space that no one ever used, Susannah was humming something by Garbage under her breath. Only when she pushed the door open did she get her game face back on. Time to be the firm but fair queen of all she surveyed again, sort out whatever the problem was, and then get back to the office to celebrate her new investor with a large glass of something smooth.

"There you are!" Babs emerged from the cellar, wiping grimy hands on an old dishtowel. In her early fifties, she was still a compact woman, formidable in every way, from her heavy make-up to her considerable curves.

"I do have an estate to run, Barbara."

"Don't you 'Barbara' me, Lady Muck."

They exchanged a brief hug before promptly laughing.

"What's going on, then, Babs? It's not like you to be rooting around at the business end of a beer barrel. I thought you had strapping young men around to do that for you?"

"Another one of the Andersen kids didn't show up for his shift. I'm short-handed again, and then all my taps went off. Now I've fixed it, but I've had to leave a half-full bar up there on a promise not to rob the place or drink it dry. I know you've got matters of corporate global dominance or whatever, but this is part of your local business, and I'm no' a miracle worker."

Time to take one for the team and boost staff morale a little.

"Right, shall I go and see to the bar while you clean yourself up?" Susannah offered. "Don't know how you get beer out of polyester, but you can always burn that top and start again."

"You should know it doesn't burn. I had a ruder phrase in mind there, but I am in the presence of a lady. Allegedly." With that, Babs flounced off towards the staff kitchen.

That left Susannah to go and face the thirsty hordes. To her surprise, there was no looting of the spirits bottles when she pushed through the swing doors to get behind the bar. Instead a few locals were in clusters at tables and booths around the place, drinks in front of them and making the usual amount of noise. The jukebox wasn't on, but the sports news played on an endless silent loop on the televisions that usually showed live football and rugby, unless the cricket fans came in and kicked up a fuss.

As soon as they saw her, the room fell silent like a saloon in an old-fashioned Western. Susannah rested her hands on her hips, defiant, and stared back at them in turn.

"Free drinks, then is it?" someone called out from the far corner. "Better stick to the bottled stuff, your Ladyship." Laughter rippled across the room, but Susannah stood her ground until one of the local farmers approached with a sheepish request for a bottle of red wine.

She turned her back on the room with its rich, dark wood panelling and its red velvet-covered seats, some more worn than others. The scent of polish lingered faintly even with a crowd drinking and snacking. The beer taps gleamed, brassy and bold, as they broke up the long, curved line of the bar that took up a whole corner of the space.

Once she handed over the wine and took the offered cash, Susannah's shoulders dropped an inch or so. Her hands stopped clenching and unclenching in search of something to occupy them. There was no real crisis to solve here; she was simply holding the fort.

They came forward in a trickle then, and a few new customers did quick double takes as they entered and saw her behind the bar. Susannah slipped her blazer off and put it over a handy stool, the better to move around.

Despite her natural tendency for drama, Babs ran a tight ship. Everything was easy to find. The prices were already programmed into the till. Save for a bit of mental arithmetic that had Susannah reaching for her phone calculator, the job was almost proving a good fit. Perhaps she'd have made a decent barmaid in another life that hadn't sent her to Marlborough College and scraping a third-class degree at Durham.

Someone cleared their throat behind her. "Hiya, can I—" The voice trailed off, uncertain.

She turned. Well, apparently the sight of Susannah behind the bar was enough to render the new vet temporarily speechless. It looked good on her. "Yes?"

"Well, uh… Sorry, are you really serving drinks?" Tess asked. "Or is this some strange local prank I'm not getting?"

Susannah gestured with both hands to emphasise where she was standing. "Well, I'd hardly be back here unless I were. Or did you think my pub had gone self-service? By all means, just come back and help yourself."

"No thanks, but I think I'll wait for Babs. I like my drinks poured properly. A real pint, none of that bottled stuff."

Well, that was just rude. Never one to back down, Susannah pulled a fresh glass from the selection by the pumps and held it up to the light for a second. Spotless. *Good.* "Let me guess: you're the weak lager type? Maybe a shandy, ease you in gently?"

"Two pints of best, actually. And an orange juice."

Susannah glanced past Tess, seeing the other two vets camped out at the table by the unlit fireplace. She swapped the tall lager glass for the stubbier ale one, remembering that much from when she'd ordered drinks for Jimmy. The trick, she was fairly sure, was to hold the glass upright with the nozzle pressed against the bottom. None of that pouring on an angle for ale. The pump was stiff, but Susannah hadn't spent as many hours in the gym and steering obstinate horses to fail on upper-body strength. She didn't realise her arm was flexing until she caught Tess watching. They shared a brief moment of eye contact, and then they both looked away.

Interesting.

"I can take it from here," Babs said, emerging in a new top as Susannah set the first pint on the bar. "Not bad, Boss. You might just be a natural."

"You get the orange juice." Susannah reached for a glass for the second pint. "I'm getting the hang of this."

"Didn't know this place was part of your, y'know..." Tess gestured with a nod.

"Estate?"

"I was going for 'empire,' but sure. You don't charge extra when you don't like someone's driving, do you?"

It was a weak attempt at breaking the ice. Susannah didn't feel like indulging it. She'd had a big win, money secured for turning Midsummer into something meaningful. Maybe that was reason enough to go easy on the new girl, but Susannah suspected any moment of weakness would only be thrown back in her face later.

She was hardly the most beloved of landowners, despite her best efforts over the years, and it wasn't as though that would be any different with Tess. Winning hearts and minds could be left to the PR firm Susannah would have to hire for the new developments on the estate. "No, but you can still tip generously."

"Right, yeah," Tess said. "I'll do that. Tip the woman who could probably buy and sell us all."

Someone had a chip on her shoulder. Still, it wouldn't be a trip into Hayleith without a spot of class war. Susannah had plenty of experience by now at playing the part of the Dickensian villain.

Tess turned to Babs to pay, making a show of shoving the change in the tip jar before retreating with her triangle of drinks gripped in both hands.

For a fleeting second, Susannah wished she didn't have a stubborn streak wider than the River Tweed. Another person might have taken the opportunity to mend fences with the newcomer whose smile was actually quite pleasant. Still, Susannah could no sooner change her nature than she could grow wings and fly herself home, so no point dwelling on the impossible. Tess was already absorbed into her little clique anyway, Susannah no doubt already chased from her thoughts.

"Thank you," Babs interrupted. "I called the Andersens; they've decided the boy isn't sick after all and he'll be down in ten minutes to cover. You can get on with your evening."

"Speaking of getting on, I need a spot of catering early next week..." It felt better to bring up a slightly awkward topic than admit that Susannah didn't really have any grand plans for her evening.

There was a heartfelt groan in response.

"Well, yes," Susannah continued. "And that response is why I'm going to ask Joan again. You know she helps me out sometimes since Francine quit on me. No problems with that, I assume?"

There was no missing the way Babs's face crumpled for just a second, but as always, she bounced right back.

"Ask whomever you like. No skin off my nose."

"Right. Of course." Susannah didn't add that it very much did affect Babs, her nose, and her ability to cry into a bottle of Pinot Grigio. One day the plan was to sit Joan and Babs down together, sort out their decade-old feud, and make catering arrangements considerably less fraught. But, as Finn had said just yesterday, some tasks were hundreds of places down the list.

"I'd best be going, then." Susannah put her jacket on and moved towards the door.

Babs was already distracted with new customers who'd just piled through the door. The local rugby club, judging by the striped tops and copious amounts of mud on each woman.

As Susannah pulled her car around onto the main street, she glanced to the big picture windows that formed the corner of the pub by the fireplace. It did look cosy, even late on a summer evening. She was just admiring her property, that was all. Nothing at all to do with the ponytailed redhead throwing her head back in laughter over her pint of bitter.

Susannah put the Land Rover back in gear and drove off towards the big, empty house waiting for her.

Chapter 5

Tess threw her vet bag into the boot of the car. The leather on the battered old thing was a little worn in places, and there were a few stains that even industrial-strength disinfectant hadn't entirely removed. She slammed the boot closed with a satisfied pat.

This was why she had moved back here, to get to the countryside and do some real vet work. The coughing hamsters and matted cats would be waiting this afternoon, but for the morning, at least, she got to roam free.

She caught sight of Adam by the front door of the surgery, no doubt on his way to give her more faintly patronising advice about how to handle "the big stuff". That had her scurrying for the driver's seat and roaring down the road before he could catch up.

The farm wasn't far outside the village, a modest smallholding with the house set far back from the main road, on the crest of a small hill. The fences were all neat and new, not as rundown as Tess remembered from when she was growing up. She drove along the track that led to a cute front garden and then came to a stop. Tess checked for other dogs before she considered letting Waffles out from the back, where he was wagging his tail like a drumbeat.

Checking the name on her tablet screen one last time, Tess hopped out onto the gravel. The moment her walking boots made contact, two things happened at once: the front door opened to reveal a tall, broad man with well-worn blue overalls and long hair that would have been more at home in a metal band, and the grey skies fulfilled their threat, sending the rain coming down in buckets.

"Come in, come in!" The man's voice was booming, enough to get Tess's feet moving before she had a chance to think about it.

"Mr Laskowska?"

"You must be the new vet I've been hearing about. You said my name right, that's a good start."

His Polish accent was faint, tinged with broad Scots. When he shook her hand, the skin was coarse but a little damp from being freshly washed.

"I picked up a little Polish here and there, so I try to pronounce it right when I see it," Tess said. "You've been having trouble with one of the ewes?"

"Yes. This rain won't last long. I can make coffee, and then we can head to the field?"

Her morning wasn't too booked, so Tess agreed without hesitation, following him into the roomy farmhouse kitchen. Instead of the country-casual woodwork she expected, the room was bright and airy, thanks to surfaces reflecting the light with shiny white finishes and a whole lot of chrome. It was something out of a magazine, and Tess couldn't help a quiet "Wow!" as she took it all in.

"You like it?"

"It's gorgeous," Tess replied. "Is this all your work, Mr Laskowska?"

He shook his head. "Call me Dave, everyone else does. No, I did the hanging and the banging, but the look is all by my partner, Finn. They're very talented." He shot her a look when using the pronoun.

Tess nodded in acknowledgement. She was aware that her sexuality could mostly be guessed at a glance. She had also learned not to make those same assumptions about gender. Things were a million miles from how it was when she was growing up, though. At least one lesbian and one non-binary person living in Hayleith? Her neighbours' heads would have exploded back then. "Well, they can come and give me some tips on my place when I finally move in. I'm staying in Margo and Adam's guest room a few more days, but this is fantastic."

"Thank you. I'll tell Finn you're another fan." Dave set about making them both coffee, and it was as good as anything the café served up.

"What's been troubling you with your sheep?" Tess sat on one of the high stools at the kitchen island. "The notes don't say much from Adam's first visit, I'm afraid."

"Her lamb is weaned now, but it looks like she's having some trouble. Usually I have some antibiotics left over to give them, but this is my best girl. I think she deserves a check from the vet and her own prescription."

Dave talked about the sheep with a smile, but there was real concern in the way he leaned in to discuss it.

That was a good start in Tess's book, since sheep were often an afterthought, and many livestock owners wouldn't go to the expense of a vet visit for sheep alone. They usually waited until something more valuable needed attention, like cows, and then asked about the sheep as a kind of bonus. "No problem. I've got a few options in my bag, so when I see how she's doing, we'll get the right one injected and she'll be back in fine form."

"That is just what I wanted. How are you settling in? I think I saw you in the pub last night?"

"Yeah, I think I saw you too," Tess sipped her coffee. "Had a bit of a run-in with our local royalty again. You must be glad to have your own place, not be working for Mrs Karlson up at Midsummer."

"You mean *Lady* Karlson?" The correction was polite, but it might also have been pointed. "We are actually her tenants. She owns this land, but we rent and work it. Very fair, of course. But then my partner sets the rates, so always a good deal, right? And Lady Karlson owns the pub too."

"I heard." Tess leaned over and put her mug in the sink. So Finn with the great taste also worked up on the estate. "Looks like the rain is easing off. Shall we go see to your poor sheep?"

"Yes, come this way."

They headed out through the back door and across to the first set of barns. The rain was down to a drizzle, and Tess's wax jacket kept the worst of it off. Back here barely a week and she was already dressing the part. Her boots were less fortunate in the squelching mud, and she remembered that the wellingtons in the car should probably be her uniform on field days like this.

"Here she is." Dave gestured to a large sheep inside the third shed along. "Thank you for coming to help her."

"Having fun?"

Margo was lurking by the surgery's back door when Tess parked. A few years ago, Margo would have been smoking, but now everyone seemed to have given up. Tess barely missed it herself.

"Oh, a great time," she replied. "Dealt with that cow who kicks more than Messi, some pigs that'd gone off their feed, and, oh yes, the sheep with sore nipples." She tried to play it down, but she could feel a smile practically splitting her face. "Think I'm meant to be a country vet after all. It was great, Margo. Absolutely why I came up here."

"Good, good." Margo looked around like she expected them to have company in the tiny car park. She'd been like that last night too, eyes darting around the pub, holding her breath every time someone came in the direction of their table.

Tess had known her too long to push for a direct explanation, though. "Did you need me to do something?" she asked, letting Waffles out to tear around the place, doing loops around their legs.

"I wanted to have a quick chat last night, but then you were all annoyed about Susannah Karlson at the bar and something about lager, so I thought it could wait until today."

"You're not firing me, are you?" Tess knew it was a pointless concern; she'd invested in the practice as an equal partner. "Only that sounds like a crap ton of paperwork, and you know that's not my strong suit."

"No it was more... Oh, hell, let's just rip it off. I'm pregnant."

Tess wanted to laugh at how stricken Margo looked. "But that's good, isn't it? You guys have been trying..."

"Yes! But we were hoping things would be more stable by the time it actually happened. As it is I'll have to step back from a lot of the job, which isn't ideal. You and Adam will have to cover for me, and we won't have the boost from new business, like Midsummer, to do any more hiring. Locums end up costing a fortune, so it'll be all on you two."

"Don't worry about that now!" Tess pulled Margo into a hug, and Waffles came bounding over to get in on the fussing. "You're having a baby!"

"Yes, I suppose I am!" Margo smiled for the first time, neon bright in her happiness. "It's been a rocky first trimester, but it's so much better now. D'you think I'm showing yet?"

Margo was so slender that Tess couldn't imagine there would be room for a child to grow in there, but sure enough, from the side there was a certain curve that Tess hadn't noticed before.

"Wow, so you're already four months?"

Margo nodded.

Tess could have sworn she saw a flicker of panic cross her face, and then, just as suddenly, it was gone. Then the part of her brain that handled the numbers kicked in with what four months meant. It meant Margo already knew when Tess was committing her whole future to this project that a baby would be throwing a lot of things up in the air. From what Margo had just been worrying about, it meant the workload and the potential financial hit would all be on Tess and Adam.

"I would have told you sooner but—"

"You were worried I wouldn't buy in," Tess finished the thought, her jaw working. "And you really needed the investment, didn't you?"

Margo shook her head, but it was far from convincing. "Most of all, I wanted to work with you. We always talked about having a practice together, but you went off to London, and, well, now we get another shot at it."

"You should have given me all the information. I deserved that much. What if Adam and I can't cope? He's going to be tired and distracted with a new kid around. Am I going to have to keep the lights on by myself?" Tess heard her voice getting louder, but she couldn't seem to rein it back in. "What happens if I can't do the work of three people? Does the practice just go under?"

"Tess, please."

"I'm going to get lunch," Tess decided, clipping Waffles back on his leash for the walk out to the street. "And I'll get over it; I know I will. I'm just going to need a minute to deal, okay?"

"Sure, of course," Margo said. "My gut instinct was always to tell you; I just want you to know that. Adam was more cautious, and then you started telling us how Caroline tied you in knots over money and lied to you about it."

"Yeah, so you know how I feel about other people sneaking around, lying to my face. Especially when it comes to information that could affect my whole life! My security, my ability to support myself… I've already thought once before that I'd be left with nothing."

Tess wouldn't have brought that up, but Margo had heard more of those complaints about Caroline than anyone else. As her best friend, Margo should have trusted Tess to make the right decision with all the facts, and she wasn't about to just let her off the hook for it right away.

The short march across the street was worth it when Tess saw mac and cheese on the daily specials board, and it earned a rumble from her unsubtle stomach. She waited out the small queue of people while Waffles availed himself of the doggy water bowls by the front door.

"Dr Robinson," Joan greeted her at the counter, but it wasn't entirely friendly, judging by the way her arms were crossed over her chest. "I've been hearing about you again."

Irrationally, all Tess could think was that she was somehow going to be denied macaroni and cheese, which, after a fight with her best friend, felt like cruel and unusual punishment. "What have you heard?" Best to brave it out. There was garlic bread cooking somewhere, so the stakes were only getting higher. "And you can just call me Tess, you know. I don't stand on ceremony."

"You've been drinking in that pub apparently. Despite my advice."

"Well, it is *right there*, Joan. I was invited, so it would have been rude not to go. The whole village was there, practically!"

"Hmph." They stared each other down, Joan's deep-brown eyes unblinking.

Tess knew she had no chance if she folded at that point, so she shoved her hands into her pockets and refused to look away.

"You eating, then?" Joan finally asked.

"Yes, please," Tess said around a quiet sigh of relief. "I'll have the macaroni, and does that come with garlic bread?"

"Might do."

"Right, then. And a fizzy drink with that, whatever you've got that's diet."

Joan nodded to indicate that Tess should take a seat.

She looked around for Waffles to bring him inside. He was well-trained but occasionally being allowed to wander around places where everyone would fuss over him made him a bit of a rebel. There was a moment's panic when Tess couldn't see him anywhere. He never wandered off without her, and there was still a road right out there, even if it was hardly a major thoroughfare.

"Come on, then," said a friendly but decidedly posh voice.

Waffles came trotting in then, the handle of his leash in his mouth like he had just brought back a kill.

"You're a handsome boy, aren't you?" the voice continued. "Who do you belong to?"

"He's mine," Tess answered, looking up from where a hand had started petting Waffles to see the last person she expected to sound so perky about a strange dog. "Oh."

"You never seem very pleased to see me, do you?" Susannah replied with the hint of a smirk. "Just as well you couldn't land my business, then, wouldn't you say?" She sauntered off to talk to Joan. It was almost strutting, really, the confidence with which she walked in those heels.

Tess gave Waffles a welcome scratch behind his ears and tried to focus on her imminent dose of carbs and cheese.

The door had barely swung closed when Margo came bursting in to join her, unable to let the disagreement fester between them. "Tess, I'm so sorry. There's no excuse, and I just want you to know I really, really apologise. And listen, if there's anything you need to see about the business, or anything you want us to do or show you, I'm more than happy to do it. You coming here has made my whole year, every bit as much as this baby. Who, by the way, I'm fully expecting you to be godmother to, come the time."

"I'm not religious, though."

"Neither are we, but it's handy for getting into the good schools." Margo hesitated after making the little joke as if to see if it was too soon.

Tess gave her a weak smile in return.

"Anyway, we'll deal with that once there's a baby out in the world. Most importantly: are we cool going forward? It wasn't about tricking you, Tess."

"You sure?"

"Of course," Margo replied. "What it really was, and I know we've sort of talked about it before, but I didn't want to make it a big deal... We've had a couple of times that, well, they didn't stick. I had to get to twelve weeks this time before I told anyone. I wouldn't have even told Adam, honestly, if he hadn't seen the pregnancy test in the bin."

"Oh, Margo." Tess got up to hug her best friend. "Say no more. We're fine. The practice is fine, and it's only going to get even better going forward. Okay?"

"You're the best, mate."

"Yeah, I know."

Susannah could have kicked herself for not remembering whose beautiful golden Lab that was, although naming him after a breakfast food was absolutely inane. There wasn't much chance she would forget now, though, not with daggers being stared into her back the entire time she talked with Joan.

The pocket-sized vet showed up, and they were soon having some hushed and emotional conversation with lots of gesturing and then hugging. Just more justification for not hiring the Sisterhood of the Travelling Stethoscope.

"I need a spot of catering," Susannah said, smiling that Joan had started on her double espresso the minute she walked through the door. "Now, it's next week, so there's no rush, but you always do a lovely spread, and it's a little beyond what Babs can manage with the pub kitchen."

"I've always said you should rip that tiny tin can of a kitchen out and start over," Joan said. "I wanted to the whole time I worked there. Make it into a nice little gastro pub. It would do good business for the town too. Bring in more people stopping on long drives."

"Yes, thank you, Joan. Always a pleasure to get a business lesson from you. But if I email you with numbers and dietary requirements today, can you fit me in for lunch next Tuesday? Morning drop-off is fine; we have the fridge space. Just sort it out with Finn as needed."

"And I suppose you got permission from Her Majesty?"

"Babs gave her blessing, yes. Not that I need it from either of you. This is just business, and we need to pull together in a small place like this."

Joan nodded. "You're really not going to make any changes to that place, even now? It's stuck in a time warp."

Susannah held her hands up, accepting the charge with a silent guilty plea. "You know how I feel about The Spiky Thistle. It's the one part of the estate that doesn't require constant upkeep, that doesn't have a to-do list a mile long. Besides, there's something to be said for preserving a little bit of our history. Jimmy always loved it just as it is."

"People would talk if they knew you were such a romantic. Preserving a whole pub in amber for the sake of your husband's memory. It's not guilt over changing everything else, is it? People have been gossiping about some of the plans that have been doing the rounds, and I thought you might have mentioned that in passing. Those of us who've run your businesses like to be in the loop. God knows Babs will expect it."

Susannah waited until the coffee changed hands. She didn't want to end up wearing it. "Not often I hear you refer to the good old days. Or acknowledging you ever were an 'us' with dear old Babs. When are you two going to finally see sense and talk to each other again?"

Joan held one hand out to the side and bent it towards the floor as though checking the temperature. "Well, it seems hell hasn't frozen over yet, so it won't be today."

"Here." Susannah handed over a five-pound note for the coffee. "Keep the change."

Joan narrowed her eyes but accepted the cash. "You send me that list before dinner, you hear? Or I might get too busy."

"I will. Thank you." It was ridiculous that Susannah had to negotiate small tasks like this, but there was bad blood between Joan and Finn that there was little point in raking over. Sometimes being the boss meant Susannah rolling up her sleeves and taking the path of least resistance; she'd learned that much in business so far.

When she was done talking with Joan, there wasn't much reason to hang around, but Susannah decided the free table in the corner was as good a place as any to set up her laptop and sip at her coffee. She was definitely not watching when Joan bustled out of the kitchen with a plate of macaroni that actually looked pretty appetising.

Susannah lost interest when the dish landed in front of Tess, aside from watching Waffles stare at it like the least Tess could have done was pick something with meat in it.

The other vet must have gone back to work.

Susannah took a long sip of her coffee, the heat on her tongue a warning shot for the jolt of caffeine her system was crying out for. Maybe it was time to start looking into rescue dogs to rehome on the estate. The stables were one big part of it, but the whole point was to provide a sanctuary for as many animals as possible. God knew Susannah had the land for it. She could start with greyhounds, though they were skinny, nervous things. She'd been around animals enough to know they trusted her, so a bit of jumpiness could probably be overcome.

Any hope of peace and quiet was shattered when Finn appeared, looking really quite agitated. The sight of a rolled-up newspaper in their hands was enough to make Susannah's stomach sink.

She glanced around, saw how many people in the café had noticed the commotion of Finn's arrival, and made a decision. "Not here."

It came out as more of a hiss. Striding out of the café, laptop under her arm, Susannah didn't have to worry about Finn following. The two of them met where both cars were parked. A drizzle was starting.

"Can we—?"

"Finn, just lay it on me. You look like there's a national shortage of hair wax."

"Don't even joke about that," Finn said. "So we submitted the plans the other day for the changes on the estate. The animal sanctuary, expanding the stables, and the new holiday cabins way on the outskirts, because we agreed that's the minimum rental income you'd need to keep everything else running."

Susannah opened the Land Rover door and tossed her things into the passenger seat.

"Well, it looks like, uh, someone has gone to the press and portrayed the plans as turning the estate into a tacky amusement park. There's a whole story about how you didn't inherit legitimately and that the estate was supposed to stay in the family. Basically—"

"All the stuff Robin has been threatening me with this past year. She's obviously got tired of waiting for me to be intimidated."

The door slam wasn't satisfying enough, but damn if Susannah didn't really put her back into it. The whole car vibrated with the force.

"It should be easy enough to shoot her down, no? Surely a word or two in the right places, a PR blitz of our own, and she'll look like the nutty old soak that she is."

Finn shrugged and handed over the newspaper with great reluctance. "There's some personal stuff too. Nothing that anyone with sense is going to give half a crap about, Suze, but it's definitely meant to come after your reputation, your marriage. The papers seem to be salivating over two ladies of a certain social status feuding through the press."

It felt like ice down her spine, a steady trickle that rendered Susannah immobile on the rough surface of the small car park. She and Jimmy had always been circumspect about their arrangement as husband and wife, and for a brief period Susannah had wondered if Robin's excessive interest in their home and business had been a ploy for Susannah's attention. She had always attracted a certain kind of interest from women still firmly in the closet. The fact that Robin might try and use all that for leverage was enough to make Susannah want to throw up her coffee right then and there. She managed to resist, if only because the riding boots she'd put on that morning were close to brand new.

"Finn, you're on damage control," she finally managed, forcing herself to seem as composed as ever. "Hit back as hard as you need to, and whatever dirt we can unearth on Robin, on the family..."

"I thought you said we weren't to go near Jimmy's legacy?"

"That was before his bloody legacy started attacking me on a daily basis. Do I look like I want to give up everything because of some mudslinging in the press? That's the evening edition, yeah?"

Finn nodded.

"Then get our version in every morning paper that'll take it. Online, social media, hand-delivered flyers if we need to. Start a blog if they haven't died off already. But I don't want to look anywhere tomorrow and see her version over mine. Understood? As far as the public knows, whatever I do with the estate now is the late lord's shared vision, and anything else would be an insult to his memory."

"You got it, Boss."

"And Finn?"

"Yeah?"

Susannah placed a hand on their shoulder, patting the starched line of Finn's blazer. "Thank you. For having my back. I couldn't do all this without you."

"Well, you must be rattled if you're throwing around compliments," Finn answered with a modest grin. "I'll nail her and Jonathan to the wall if I have to. Did you get the catering sorted in there? Maybe we should prioritise getting you another chef."

"No, Joan will do it for now." Susannah did her best to hide how tempted she was. "All about supporting local business, remember? It tends to stop them showing up at the door with pitchforks and flaming torches."

"How very *Beauty & the Beast* of you."

"I'd better get back to the office. I have a ton of calls to make. And Finn? This is probably a good time to get the missing staff positions filled. We're going to need all hands on deck."

"You've got that vet coming in this afternoon too." Finn glanced over to where Tess was exiting the café, Waffles back on his leash. "I think he works out of the Jedburgh branch, but they're all over the place."

"Big firm. That's what we'll need for such a big project."

"Right."

"Right."

Finn headed back to their car, a nippy little GT with a souped-up engine, and Susannah waited until it had roared out onto the street before walking around and getting in her own car. Before starting it, she watched Tess jogging around with Waffles, the happy dog barking his head off, and wondered what it might be like not to have the weight of the world on her shoulders every day.

No doubt that was her unbearable privilege talking, as Babs had once called it. Susannah had no intention of trading her stately home and investment portfolio for an easier life, one with just a single rent to worry about. Still, it didn't stop her wondering what it might be like to get up and meander through a day without properties needing maintenance or tenants to chase for late payments.

She glanced down at the article and decided not to grant it space in her head for the moment. Self-pity could come later. She had work to do.

Susannah was waiting on the driveway to greet the arriving vet. She hadn't bothered to change, since the interview, such as it was, would require a good walk around the existing stables and the areas Susannah planned to develop to house more animals. She had her riding boots and jodhpurs on, though she hadn't had a chance to get out for a ride today. Maybe that explained the restless feeling in her bones. A day of waging war in the press and over the phone had left her yearning for an hour out in the fields with only the wind and a horse's soft grunts for a soundtrack.

Her blouse was silk, expensive, and that creamy colour that only seemed to happen above a certain price range. It crushed a little under her heavy wax jacket, but it was too brisk outside still for anything less.

"Thanks for coming," she said, extending a hand to the vet.

The tall, bearded man in his fifties shook it with enough force to dislocate an elbow.

Susannah wrung her fingers free as quickly as she could. At least he had the rough skin of someone who actually worked for a living.

"No bother, lass. Bit of a drive for our practice, but it sounds like you'll be needing someone here full-time, eh? That should make it worth our while."

"That might be necessary in the future, yes." Susannah kept her tone light, but she could already tell this man hadn't read the detailed briefing she'd had Finn send out for firms to quote on. "I'd like to start with the current commitments, though. If you'd like to follow me?"

The entire walk down to the stables, Susannah endured a torrent of mansplaining about everything from how the hedges were trimmed to the type of gravel that made up the paths.

"Right," she finally interrupted as they got to the stables, "we can start with my own horse. This is Billie Jean."

It was hard not to be proud of the striking chestnut, just under sixteen hands high. Billie Jean whinnied softly at the sight of Susannah by the stable door.

"That's quite a choice of name," the vet remarked. "Women are so inventive about these things, but I'm more of a traditionalist."

"My late husband named her. She was a wedding gift to welcome me to my new home. Jimmy was quite the tennis fan. Almost went professional as a young man."

"Ah. Right. May I…?"

He didn't wait for the okay before opening the door and stepping into her stall.

Billie Jean huffed at the intrusion, so Susannah gave her a reassuring stroke down her long muzzle. Clearly neither of them was very impressed so far.

"She's had a tough life, this one. Her legs look a bit overworked," Mr Vet called from somewhere near the back. Susannah had already forgotten his name.

"She was a racer," she replied. "She has a light load here, though, plenty of gentle exercise."

"Don't like the look of these fetlocks," he continued, stroking various parts of the horse without waiting to see how she reacted to each one. "Have you thought about her lifespan?"

Susannah patted Billie Jean more forcefully, resisting the urge to hug the big girl. "She's been perfectly fit since she came here. Listen, perhaps we should move on to the others? There are four horses stabled here for now, with room for at least a dozen more. Unless you're ready to just write them off now?"

"No, I can inspect them. But thoroughbreds come with their own complications; I'm sure you know that. I know you probably left the care and maintenance to the stable hands growing up, but you'll have picked up some bits along the way."

Susannah gave him a tight smile as he reappeared, slapping Billie Jean on the flank as if she were a second-hand car he was trying to sell. There was little doubt that this working relationship would be unbearable, but the trouble with a big country estate was that it was only near to so many places, and only a few of those had large veterinary practices.

"Okay, let me show you McEnroe," Susannah said. "And for the record, I did grow up riding, but my parents always had me take care of my own horses too. We didn't just defer to the staff."

He shot her a smug look that said anyone with staff wouldn't know the first thing about mucking out horses, and Susannah was tempted to grab a pitchfork and start tossing some hay around on principle. Did people really think a title meant she'd never lifted her hand to an honest day's work?

The rest of their conversation was downhill from there, but mercifully short. Mr Vet seemed unshakeably confident that he had the estate's business as he got back into his truck.

Susannah ran her hands over her hair in frustration before heading back into the house.

"Well?" Finn said as soon as Susannah entered the home office. "Does that solve all your problems?"

"I think it's our only choice, but I'm going to sleep on it another night."

"But you said—"

"And now I'm saying I want to sleep on it. There are other priorities, Finn. Get me a chef and enough farmhands to handle the work we already have." Susannah started to build into a ranted to-do list.

Finn grabbed a tablet and started typing.

Susannah caught herself, and took a deep, deep breath. "Sorry. I know you're on top of it. That man, though… I want to believe we can do better than a patronising old git." Susannah threw her hands up in despair as she collapsed into her desk chair.

"You know what I'm going to suggest, but I don't want you taking my head off, so it can wait until tomorrow."

"Thanks, Finn. I'll be in a better mood then."

Finn stopped on the way out of the office. "Sure about that?"

"Well, no. But I live in hope." Susannah waved Finn off and turned back to the next problem in the stack.

"Morning!" Margo called out from the staff room. She held a mug of something that smelled herbal and yucky, and a sticky bun the size of her head. Beyond greeting Tess, she seemed engrossed in a couple of newspapers spread out across the table. "Glad you decided not to hate me, by the way."

"You look like you're tracking down a murderer in an old-fashioned cop show." Tess, holding her travel mug of piping-hot coffee, took a seat. It was a nice space to hang out in—some kind of storage room converted into a spacious kitchen area once the vets took over. The walls were exposed brick with huge windows that looked out over fields. The table they were sharing was large enough to seat ten, but there had never been that many people to fill the seats. "And I could never hate you. I was just a bit thrown."

"I know. Now this is way more interesting than Miss Marple antics," Margo said, not quite looking up. "The Karlsons are airing their dirty laundry in public, and honestly I never thought I'd see the day. I mean, there have been rumours around here for years about that marriage…"

"As long as you're feeling okay and the baby is okay," Tess continued before her brain caught up with her mouth. "Wait, the *Karlsons*? As in—"

"Our local upper classes?" Margo smirked as she pushed a folded newspaper over to Tess. "You'll want to start with that story as it seems to have kicked off some drama yesterday."

"Why is everything since I moved here about this Karlson woman?" Tess looked at the picture before reading the article. It was from some kind of county show with horses and rosettes and an unfortunate-looking vicar trying to play master of ceremonies. It must have been a few years back, because Susannah looked younger. Her hair was shorter, one of those bobs with bouncy curls that was fashionable for a while. More make-up than the other times Tess had seen her, dressed for the occasion instead of her usual rotation of riding clothes and business suits. Not that she was keeping a mental portfolio or anything. She just noticed things, that was all.

"Lady Karlson, and don't you forget it. That's how she signed her press release, apparently, even though she's always made a show of not using her title. It's always 'Call me Susannah.' like it makes her one of the common people."

"She doesn't sound very common to me. Does anyone really fall for that?"

"Most of the people round here are just flattered when the rich lady pays them some attention, in case there's a job or something else they might get out of it. And it's not like she's new money, either. It didn't all come from the husband."

"I thought she married into it," Tess said as she started to dig into the article. It was just a local rag, the same one that had covered the area since she did her paper round in a village not so different to this one twenty years ago. If she concentrated, Tess could still feel the stretch in her calves from all the hills she gleefully biked her way up and down to drop off a few sheets of easily smeared ink on cheap paper. "But I guess it doesn't matter how you get it, as long as you have it. I wouldn't go around calling myself by some title, though, but then I'd never marry posh, would I?"

"It's different for lesbians anyway." Margo shifted in her seat as though she was about to deliver one of her very special moments. They were old, dear friends, but Margo really should have been a teacher of some sorts with the way she loved to explain things to an audience, willing or not.

"How so?"

"Well, when a man is knighted—made a sir and all that jazz—then his wife gets to use the title of Lady His-Surname. There's no equivalent for a same-sex couple. If your future wife is made a Dame, your wife doesn't get to use Lady. Then it's different again if it's inherited. Baronesses, marquesses… Didn't you learn all this in school?"

"No, we learned about all the times Scotland went to war with England, not how to become a duke. Who knew the ancient institutions were so behind the times, eh?" Tess asked, but her attention was already being pulled back to the article. There was a lot of speculation and innuendo. Some of it must have been treading a thin line on slander unless there was actual proof somewhere to go with it. "I've never been that impressed by royal families and titles. Give me democracy any day."

"Have you got to the bit about her 'salacious past with women'?" Margo chimed in next. "Did she, y'know, ping on your gaydar?"

"Can't say I was even considering it." Although in truth, she did usually know when someone interested or available was taking her measure. "Anyway, I don't think Susannah Karlson is the type to let anyone know her business. This must have pissed her off in a hundred different ways."

"Not as much as that very vague hint of an implication that maybe Lord James didn't pass from entirely natural causes. It's just enough to be deniable, but most people will just read their first impression. Now, say what you will about the Karlsons, but I never got the vibe they didn't care about each other. Seemed quite happy, whatever the rumours said."

Tess closed the paper and put it to one side, feeling a little queasy. She'd never cared for gossip, especially the hurtful kind. She had experienced way too much of it on the receiving end, first as the daughter of a single mother in a small town and then as a young gay woman in a place that had no template to fit her. "What's the other paper saying? More of the same?" Tess resolved not to read it if so.

"No, Karlson's defending herself. Talking about moving forward, the future of Midsummer Estates and how the only person who'll steer that is her. I almost like her for it. She's stuck two fingers up at that sister-in-law of hers, anyway."

"Robin is Karlson's late husband's sister?"

"Yeah. She brought one of her West Highland terriers in to us one time, not long after we opened the practice. She fed the poor thing a diet that would have killed off Henry VIII. When we suggested she avoid rich food and spoiling him, she picked up the dog and marched right out. We sent an invoice for the appointment fee, but she never paid."

Tess checked her watch, which doubled as her step counter and general bleeping reminder of everything important in her life, and saw that her first appointment was almost due. "Says a lot about a person, how they treat their animals. And how animals treat them. And whatever else she's done,

Susannah seems to have made a good impression on Waffles. He's all over her whenever she appears."

"Well, with the best will in the world, Tess, that dog isn't going to be joining Puppy Mensa any time soon, is he?"

Tess laughed, watching Waffles tear around the field outside. She would bring him back into the surgery between appointments, get him fed, and let him flop out in the big dog basket in the corner of the staff room. "Are you calling my dog thick?"

"I'm saying you only have him because he flunked out of guide dog school. Was he the one who kept trying to lead people into traffic?"

"No! That was his sister, Pancake. Waffles was the one who got too excited to pay attention every time he met a new trainer. So, yeah, you might have a point. He's not exactly discerning."

"What about you? You don't seem quite so anti-Karlson as you did in the pub the other night."

Tess shrugged. "I don't care much either way, but I don't think anyone deserves that kind of thing written about them. I know you find small-town stuff quaint, but for me growing up here, even one line of that in the parish newsletter would have destroyed me. Still, she's probably made of sterner stuff."

"And has her millions to console her if she's not," Margo added. "What's up first for you?"

"Spot of neutering." Tess put her coffee mug in the dishwasher and washed her hands. "We'll catch up later, yeah?"

Margo nodded, already back to reading the paper.

Tess took off down the corridor, trying desperately not to think about Susannah Karlson and "relationships with women" in the same sentence. That just sounded like a whole lot of trouble, and that was the last thing that Tess needed.

After lunch, Tess took great delight in loading up her car again. She'd managed to get two local farms not currently using their vet services to agree to a meeting, so she was going to get out there and drum up enough business to make this practice the success it needed to be.

She headed out along the long and winding roads, sticking just below the speed limit because she didn't trust herself with country driving yet. Still, it was a damn sight easier than dealing with the M25.

Her phone bleeped from where it sat charging in its little dock and providing her some slightly better GPS directions than the car's system did. No more ending up stuck on the wrong access road. Tess couldn't have endured the mockery. She tapped to answer the call via Bluetooth, and an unexpected voice greeted her.

"Hi Tessie, how are you?"

"Caroline?" It took considerable white-knuckled control not to swerve off the road. "Is everything okay? Why are you calling?"

"No reason. Well, I've got some post here for you, and I couldn't find your forwarding address. Doesn't look urgent, but I thought you might want it."

"Yeah, sure. I'm driving just now, but I'll email you the address." The same address that Tess had already sent by text, email, and left on a Post-it with her keys when she finally left London. "I'm sure you're busy."

"No, I've got time. What about you, Tessie? Keeping out of trouble?"

Tess gritted her teeth. She couldn't remember how the Tessie thing came about, but it never seemed to go no matter how many times she said she hated it. "Run off my feet, actually. New life, new job and all that."

"Oh, that's a little...well, you know. As long as you're filling the time, I suppose. As for me, well, I have a little news, and I thought you should hear it from me."

Great. No doubt she had franchised their old practice, or won the lottery, or some other stroke of luck that would make Tess feel sick to her stomach. And how patronising? To just assume all Tess had was her job. Caroline wasn't wrong, but she was definitely bloody condescending about it. "Do tell."

"Well, it's all very quick, I know, but I *did* meet someone. We're, uh, well, best to just rip it off I suppose? We're engaged."

Tess expected she would feel like she'd been punched. Any second. Instead there was a sort of dull, echoing *nothing* that was somehow even worse. "Sorry, did you say *engaged*? You, Caroline, who calls marriage—let me get this right—'a trap for the dimwitted bourgeoisie'...you're getting married?"

"Now, don't be like that. Bitter doesn't look good on you, Tessie. I just didn't want you to hear it from our friends first."

"I don't talk to *our* friends, remember?" Tess took the turning for the first farm she was visiting, relieved she would soon have an excuse to hang up. "You saw to that when you turned them all against me, even though you were the one who cheated and almost ruined our business without telling me."

"Oh, here we go again." Caroline sighed. "I know being single can be such a drag, but you have to look on it as an opportunity."

"Who said I was single?"

"Aren't you?"

"Did you think I moved halfway across the country to be on my own?" *Uh oh. Where the hell did that come from?* Tess was well aware of her flaws, but she wasn't generally a liar. She stopped the car when the track widened into a parking area. "Anyway, it's new, and I don't really want to talk about it to everyone yet."

"Oh, come on. Details please. Assuming she's even real," Caroline scoffed. "I mean, talk about convenient timing."

"I'm not that bothered about keeping up with you, and it's not like I'm engaged to her or anything. We are having a very nice time, though."

"And her name?"

"Susannah. Well, of course you don't know her," Tess said, wondering where in the hell *that* name just came from. No, of course, it was perfectly rational. It was just because everyone at work had been talking about Lady Karlson all day. Besides, Margo's name was no use because she and Caroline had met. Joan sounded like an old woman's name, and Babs sounded entirely made up. "But we're just seeing where it goes for now."

"Susann-ah?"

"That's…what I said." Tess was blushing redder than the checks on her plaid shirt. "Anyway, I've just arrived at a farm. Work to do!"

"Right, right. Wouldn't want to keep you from frolicking in a meadow or whatever you get up to there. Anyway, if you feel up to it, you can always pop down for the wedding. I always think it's healthier when exes do that. Real closure, you know?"

Tess glared at the phone. It was getting harder to remember why she ever liked Caroline in the first place, let alone loved her. "Yeah, sure. Shoot me an invitation. Gotta go!"

She ended the call and hit her head against the steering wheel a couple of times. What was wrong with her lately? Maybe moving into her own place would set her right again, get a bit of stability back.

With one last bang of her head for good luck, Tess accidentally sounded the horn. It sent birds scattering from a nearby tree and startled the old farmer who was walking towards the car. Not a great start.

She grabbed her bag and jumped out. Time to turn the day around.

Chapter 6

AFTER A JAM-PACKED MORNING, SUSANNAH decided on an indulgent afternoon ride to clear her head. Billie Jean was no trouble to saddle up and get going, having one of the sweetest dispositions that Susannah had ever been around.

"Come on, girl," Susannah urged her horse as they got back on the flats on the far west of the estate. There was nothing much out this way, just a meandering route to the old Edinburgh road that nobody used much anymore, and a few scattered farms that weren't part of the estate. Maybe it was time to reach out again, buy them out and keep the families on as tenants. It was something Jimmy had talked about, and it was certainly possible without derailing her own plans. Or maybe it was time to accept that she had enough on her plate instead of looking for trouble.

Billie Jean ate up the easy ground with her long strides, and Susannah bobbed in a perfect rhythm with her. The breeze was whip-fast and crisp as it came at Susannah, a refreshing smack in the face when her waning attention levels needed it most. The sun had struggled out from behind the clouds, and it made all the difference to the rolling greenery that expanded in every direction. This was the place Susannah had fallen in love with.

The ground became patchier as they skirted the edge of the farthest field from the house, marked with a big red boundary line on all the maps up in the office.

"Whoa, bring it down," Susannah urged, tugging on Billie Jean's reins to slow her to a brisk canter. "Don't want you overdoing it. We need to go back too, remember?"

As always, the horse responded like she understood English perfectly. There was never any need to tell her twice or override any willful attempts to do the opposite. It was only as they approached the next gate that the poor girl slowed down without prompting, almost limping to a stop.

Panicked, Susannah slid right out of the saddle, landing hard on her feet. Her first priority was lightening the load if Billie Jean was in any pain.

"What's up, Billie?"

The horse whinnied softly, but that didn't tell Susannah much of anything. Patting gently, Susannah made her way from one side, up around Billie's head and back down the other. Checking the fetlocks, she swore under her breath about the mansplaining vet. If anything, Billie Jean was favouring one of her front legs, the hoof hovering just above the grass.

"Let's get you some help, hmm? Stay here for me, okay?"

The reins looped around the gatepost probably weren't necessary, but Susannah knew that injured horses were more prone to being spooked or acting erratically. She pulled out her phone only to be greeted with a complete lack of signal.

Great. Just great.

Surveying her options, Susannah reckoned the nearest farmhouse was a safer bet than wandering around trying to get reception on her phone. There were cars in the drive, a couple of bodies moving around in a field with the cows, so some kind of help was at hand. It was really just across the road and a bit of a jog from here.

"I won't move you just in case." Susannah pressed her face against Billie Jean's muzzle. "You stay here, old girl, and I'll bring us help."

She took one last look, trying to reassure herself the leg wasn't broken. Although there had been so many advances, a bad break was still a death sentence for a horse, especially one who'd been ridden hard for racing. There was no way of telling how much damage Billie Jean was already carrying, but Susannah couldn't bear the thought of losing her. The horse might just have been her closest friend, apart from Finn. That was sadder than she wanted to consider.

It only took a few minutes to get to the cars, and Susannah's stomach plummeted as she recognised the sporty SUV. Of all the vets in all the world...

She couldn't even turn back now, because Tess and the farmer who owned the land were almost back at the cars too. They must have cut back across as Susannah had been heading up the long path.

"You here alone?" Susannah asked Tess, and it came out much too haughty. *Damn it.* She was never going to quite get the hang of being one of the people at this rate. Most times she didn't overly care, but it mattered when it was Billie Jean's health on the line.

"Excuse me, Mr Framingham. I think Lady Karlson here wants a word with me." Tess drew out the "lady" to at least four syllables, all of them mocking.

"Your Ladyship." Mr Framingham doffed his dirty baseball cap, bowing low with a reprimanding glance at Tess for not doing the same, leaving Susannah faintly embarrassed. Usually she didn't notice little things like that, but being around this blasted vet felt like being under a microscope.

"All right, all right," Susannah said. "Listen, I happen to have a horse gone lame on me in the field down there." She gestured, aware that her arm was flailing a little. "I need a vet, and I haven't got even a bar of signal. I'm sure you can see my predicament."

"Well, she's all done with me for now," Mr Framingham said, offering Tess up like a bouquet of flowers he didn't want. "But we'll be seeing you soon, Dr Robinson. Thanks for your help with that calf. I've never seen it handled with so little fuss. I'll be telling the boys about you when we go for a pint on Friday, you mark my words."

"Any time." Tess shook his hand, and he ambled off.

"So, you can be professional, then?" Straight to bitchy again. Susannah needed to give herself a good shake sometimes.

"With a paying customer, yes. He's joining the practice, unlike some people. Why don't you go up to his house and call your big swanky vet company? Since I'm much too small time for you, Your Ladyship. Is that the correct term of address, by the way? Should I curtsey?"

Susannah wondered if it still counted as a curtsey should she shove Tess face-first into the muck to help her on her way. Shaking her head, she forced the focus back where it belonged: on her injured horse. "Susannah is fine. Lady Karlson, if you absolutely must. The curtsey won't be necessary, but I have a horse limping that I really don't want to have put down. If you're up for it now, then I'll do whatever you want to make up for the past...rejection. Name your price."

Tess sighed. It was as though she was offended at the very mention of money, when she was the one who brought up paying customers first.

"All right, let's go. What's this horse of yours called?" She took her vet bag and strode off in the right direction.

Susannah scrambled a little to keep up with Tess. It wasn't often anyone outpaced her, so it was impressive and irritating in turn. Tess really was quite solid in that country sort of way. Her jeans weren't the skinny kind Susannah preferred but the sensible and durable sort, with plenty of pockets down the side before they disappeared into a new-looking set of green Hunter wellies. A classic, at least. Topped off with a red-and-navy checked shirt and a wax jacket, with that ubiquitous ponytail, Tess looked almost presentable. There was a term for it that Finn mentioned not so long ago. *Lumberjane*? It was definitely in that region.

"The horse?" Susannah repeated, realizing she hadn't answered yet. "Oh, right. Billie Jean."

"Is not your lover?" Tess replied, slowing her pace just enough that Susannah didn't feel she was pushing herself to keep up.

"Sorry, what?"

"Ah, thought you were a Michael Jackson fan," Tess replied. "You know, like the song?"

Susannah shook her head again. "No, she's named after the tennis player. My late husband had a thing for Wimbledon. It's silly."

"Kind of cute, actually. You won't believe some of the names we come across in a vet practice. I think my favourite so far is Voldetort. Oh," Tess said as Susannah stared, uncomprehending, "he was a tortoise. That's a *Harry Potter* reference. You're really not into pop culture, huh?"

They didn't say anything more until they reached the gate where Billie Jean was waiting with her trademark patience.

Susannah reached out to reassure her before they did anything else. "Here she is," she said when she knew Billie Jean was settled. "She's a good filly, you know."

"You're a grand dame, that's what you are, Billie Jean," Tess said, and it had none of the mockery she'd lavished on Susannah's title. Whatever her other flaws, Tess Robinson clearly knew a fine horse when she saw one. "You might be even posher than your owner here, thoroughbred like you."

Susannah wasn't sure whether to be offended or relieved, but she swallowed a sigh regardless. "You know your horses, then?"

"I trained as an equine specialist. Just didn't get enough of a chance to use it in London and ended up more as a sort of domestic animal GP. But horses are why I'm a vet. I'd see so many people riding around when I was growing up, and I always wanted to be one of them. I'd bring sugar cubes and mints to the ones up at the riding school nearest to us."

"I bet the instructors loved you for that."

"Oh, I didn't take lessons. Bit out of our price range and then some. It was just me and my mum, so we had to make do a lot. I have learned to ride since, of course. But you don't need to ride to give them treatment, thankfully."

There was a confidence about Tess that came across in everything she did. Anyone who had tussled with Susannah usually kept their distance afterwards, but Tess seemed to just keep on being exactly how she was, almost like she expected the world to adjust around her. Susannah knew she was guilty of expecting exactly that herself, but she wasn't quite used to it in someone from Tess's background.

"Can you tell if it's broken?" Susannah pointed to the injured leg. "If she's suffering, if I'm being cruel to her, you must tell me. I don't care about the size of the bill either way, but I won't see her dragged through agony just to rack up the costs."

"Whoa, whoa!" Tess held up her hands like she was surrendering to the police. "A little cynical right off the bat there."

Susannah pinched the bridge of her nose. Why was she always at her worst with people lately? This was Robin's influence. The last thing she wanted to do was be as hateful as her sister-in-law had turned out to be. Time to nip that in the bud.

"Sorry, sorry. I meant no stain on your character. I'm sure you're beyond reproach."

"Okay, Jane Austen. Apology accepted," Tess replied with a deep chuckle. It was a surprisingly pleasant sound. She bent down to inspect Billie Jean's leg, patting and soothing her the whole time, with just as much care as Susannah would show herself. Not a bad start. Thorough too.

After that initial examination, she didn't just take Susannah's word but inspected all four legs with the same laser focus. Then the hips were subject to very careful prodding, and there was the requisite general check of heart, eyes, ears, and nose. Maybe it was to prove a point. Either way, there was a certain diminishing of the tension in Susannah's shoulders when nothing was rushed or skimmed over.

"Well, your fancy vet might see something I've missed, and if you really want, we have the portable X-ray back at the surgery. But I'm confident from how she's holding herself and how she's distributing the weight that we're not looking at a break."

"How sure?"

"Sure as I can be. I'd be confident walking her back at a trot too. You might prefer the horse box, if it doesn't stress her too much. Every horse is different."

"She's not bothered by it," Susannah said with another pat for Billie Jean. "She would have been in and out of them daily from a foal. Just muscle memory to her now, no stress."

"That's usually the case with racehorses, unless they've had a bad experience stuck in the box for too long. She really is a beauty. If you've got stables full of horses like her, then I really am kicking myself that we missed out on your business. I'd be quite happy in with her all day. We'd do some good work together."

"Yes. Well. I can call someone to bring the horse box down to take it easy on her. What can I do for her in the meantime? She's clearly hurting."

"I've got some support bandaging here and an anti-inflammatory that will bring the irritation right down. She'll need cooling treatments for a few days—compresses for a while, then the bandaging goes back on. Total rest for a week, then gradual return to exercise. Think your grooms can handle that?"

"I need to hire a new one, a specialist, but the existing staff are good," Susannah replied, trying not to go on the defensive. "And, of course, they'll have a dedicated vet."

"Lucky horses," Tess said. "Right, can you keep her occupied up front while I work my magic, for now? She's much less likely to kick or try to bolt that way. Then, once you cross the road and go up a bit, the signal comes back so you can call your staff."

Right. Phone reception. Why hadn't Susannah thought to check for that when she set off to get help? Amateur hour, honestly. "Come on, Billie

Jean," she coaxed. "The vet here is going to fix you right up, and we'll be out riding again in no time."

"That's right," Tess agreed, and for some reason, while she was down on the grass spraying something cold on the horse's leg, she glanced up at Susannah and smiled.

It had to be said, it was a very nice smile indeed.

Chapter 7

Tess didn't mean to grin up at Susannah like an idiot, but there was something about the moment that dragged a smile right across her face. Perhaps just that it was the first moment between them that hadn't felt like the start of a fight, or just because calm was the best environment to treat good old Billie Jean in. Whatever the reason, it worked.

Treatment didn't take long, and Tess waited patiently with the horse while Susannah went across the road to place her call. In all the time they'd been working together, not a single car or tractor had passed. Apart from the farm she'd just visited, only a few empty buildings dotted the landscape—barns no longer used in fields that no longer yielded a crop to store.

This really was one of the more remote parts of the area, the kind of place Tess only uncovered as a child by walking much farther than she was allowed. They hadn't had a car for a long stretch, and when they did make that purchase as a family, it had been one failing rust bucket after another. It was part of why she liked her new, flash car with all the bells and whistles. There was security in being able to buy the best of stuff, and Tess had thrown her whole life into getting that security for herself.

"I can follow you up to the estate and check on her once she's stabled," Tess said once Susannah rejoined her. The sun was actually getting to be warm, beating down on them. Tess pulled herself up on the nearest stretch of wall to sit and properly bask in it.

Susannah joined her after checking in on the horse. "Don't you have other clients to visit? Sheep stuck in fences, that kind of thing?"

"Nobody around here would call a vet for that. A labourer, maybe."

"You sound like you would know," Susannah replied. "Because you're local, I mean," she added when Tess shot her a confused look.

"Sort of, yeah," Tess said. "I grew up about thirty miles from here, but I was off to Glasgow and London as soon as I could get there. I'm sure you know the story—running off to the big city to make a name for yourself and all that."

"That wasn't quite how I did it," Susannah replied. "And you shouldn't believe everything you read in the papers."

"I wasn't— I didn't..." Tess knew she shouldn't have opened her mouth. Just when things had seemed to be on an even keel, she'd thrown a cat among the pigeons all over again. Maybe it was time to consider a career where she didn't have to interact with people. At least animals weren't easily offended. Except cats, of course.

"It's fine." Susannah waved her hand, dismissing the whole topic as if it were just a delicate mist that had settled for a moment and then moved on. "Some people don't get on with their in-laws. Mine want to rob me of every penny and drag my name through the mud in the process. It is what it is."

"So, all lies, then?" Tess didn't mean to sound hopeful; she swore she didn't.

"Not all of it, no. Just the worst possible take on a set of facts, as usual. That's all the media is now, really—a bunch of people trying to be the most controversial and bending the truth until it snaps."

"I think I was right when I called you a cynic. And for what it's worth, I'm sure nobody reads that stuff. Today's news is tomorrow's recycling and all that."

"You don't have to be nice to me because of some misguided idea about customer service. I'll pay your bill regardless."

"Do people only talk to you about money or something? A person could really take offence at how you think that's all I care about. No, I get it, I'm just staff. I was only trying to make conversation, but I can get in my car and leave this to your actual vet anytime you like."

Tess didn't usually get this snippy, but the conversation with Caroline and all her ex's half-assed self-pity was still ringing in her ears. That and some residual guilt for dropping Susannah's name inappropriately a little while ago was making for a very odd mood all round.

"No, no. That won't be necessary, sorry. I truly didn't mean any offence. I...appreciate the company. It can feel like the ends of the earth out here sometimes."

Tess nodded. "It always seemed to go on forever when I was growing up. Then I got on a bus and found out what distance really was."

"You like to travel?"

"I was obsessed for a while." Tess figured it was just making conversation. "And living in London, the world's on your doorstep. A different trip every weekend, if you put everything you have into it."

"Sounds nice. I always wanted to travel more. But responsibilities… It's one week away in the summer each year, and that has to be enough."

"More than some people get, I suppose."

"Quite." Susannah looked down at her hands, clasped loosely in her lap as she leaned against the wall near where Tess sat. "Do you always wear your hair like that?"

"Like what?" Tess moved a defensive hand up to her ponytail. "What's wrong with it?"

"I didn't say there was anything wrong with it. I just wondered if you ever wear it down. When I tie my hair up all day, it gets this line through it. It made me think of that."

"Well, on workdays, yes. Trust me, you don't want it falling in your face during surgery."

"That makes sense."

"So glad you approve, Your Ladyship. But on weekends, in the evenings? Depends on how I'm feeling, I guess. Or who I'm with."

Susannah looked over at her then, and the way she raked her gaze up and down so slowly was an unasked question in its own right. Despite the urge to blurt something out, Tess stayed silent and just let it happen. That seemed to satisfy something in Susannah.

They sat for a companionable few minutes in silence, watching Billie Jean gingerly moving as little as possible. Before long, a flatbed truck came grunting along the road, towing a high silver horse box behind it.

Tess supposed she shouldn't be surprised that Dave from the other day was the one driving. He'd already shown that he was loyal to the Karlson estate.

"Riding your horses too hard?" he joked with Susannah even as he went straight to Billie Jean to check her over. "Looking for a holiday, old girl?"

"Hey! She's not that old," Susannah said. "Thank you for doing this. My own grooms both have their hands full in the paddock. I didn't want to leave her here waiting for them." Susannah paused and glanced over to Tess, then back to Dave. "Oh, sorry, this is, uh—it's Tess isn't it?"

"We've met," Tess replied, shaking Dave's hand despite her annoyance about Susannah pretending to fumble for her name. Heaven forbid she be seen slumming it with the help, right? "I'll leave you both to it. I'll get my car and follow you back to the stables, if that's okay?"

"Okay?" Dave answered, looking to Susannah for confirmation. "She'll be good?"

"As long as you two can get her in the box between you. If not, I can stay here and help," Tess said.

Susannah wasn't looking at her anymore. "No, we'll manage. You're right, you should go and get your car."

Tess trudged off to do exactly that, getting another burst of unplanned exercise as she jogged up the long track. At least this job meant she wouldn't need a gym membership.

By the time she got her car back down the lane, still a little out of breath, the horse box was loaded and ready. Like a strange little procession, they set off for the estate and its practically mythical stables.

They seemed to cover half of the Scottish Borders getting back. If she'd known, Tess might have asked for snacks and a pee break. She parked in front of the house and jumped out, ready to see what other fine horses might be stashed away up here. It was only when she turned into the courtyard that the full scale of the Midsummer Estate hit her.

This place was massive. Huge. Buckingham Palace wished it had grounds like these. The whole village could have fit in it fifty times over and still had room for a second pub. Tess let out a low whistle without quite meaning to.

Dave walked up just in time to catch her in the act. "Impressive, right?"

"It's beautiful." Tess was quite sincere about that. The gardens were immaculate, and each view was more beautiful than the next. That was even before she started on the imposing wooden structures that formed the stables and barns. The house itself was too much to take in on top of all that.

"This way." Dave jerked his head in the direction of big wooden doors that had been pinned open. "You can't miss them."

He wasn't wrong about that. Long before Tess saw Susannah brushing down Billie Jean, she heard the unmistakable stomping and snorting of stabled horses. The place was as neat as she'd ever seen, barely a stray piece of straw out of place. With a high roof, there was more light than a lot of stables would bother with, but at the stall level the horses were kept in a nice, gentle glow. There were four of them spread across six stalls, with Billie Jean the farthest from where Tess stood. A couple of quiet stablehands went about their work, one hosing down the empty stalls and the other rubbing oil into some reins and saddles.

"She seems comfortable," Tess said, approaching Susannah. "And you've given her plenty of room to rest, so that's good." While horses could sleep standing up, for their real rest they liked to lie down like most other animals.

"I just want to make sure she can get up and down okay before I leave her." Susannah reached into a bag by the door and withdrew an apple.

"Here." Tess gestured for her to hand it over. She pulled out the penknife she kept in her jeans pocket and made short work of slicing it up.

Susannah watched every movement like a hawk.

"Saves Billie Jean having to do all the work herself." Tess handed the sliced apple back.

With a couple of chunks of apple laid flat on her palm, Susannah offered it to the horse, fingers tilted down, out of accidental biting range. Teeth that size were no joke if they chomped down on a pinky finger.

It provided distraction enough for Tess to root around in her own bag, stuffed with fresh supplies from the car. After a bit of magic with antiseptic wipes later, she had a syringe ready to go. "This will give her a painkiller that lasts about forty-eight hours, and enough anti-inflammatory for the week. That should be enough for her whole recovery, but any signs of discomfort and I can come back out. Or you can let the other vet guys know, whichever."

"What do you need me to do?"

"Stand with me and keep hold of her; it's safer than having her tied. You keep her attention, and I'll be as gentle as I can with the needle. Base of the neck should be the least fuss all round."

"I've had other vets go with the rump." There was a challenge in there.

"Only for longer courses of treatment with multiple injections," Tess replied. "This should be one and done." She smoothed her hand down the side of Billie Jean's long neck, mentally tracing the triangle within which it was safe to inject. The muscles used as markers were well-defined, so Tess injected efficiently and as gently as possible.

Billie Jean neighed a little but barely flinched.

"She trusts you," Susannah said.

Damn, how did Her Ladyship get quite so close?

Susannah still had a soothing hand on her horse. "She's a patient girl, but that's calm even for her."

"All part of the job," Tess said, taking an instinctive step back just to feel like she could breathe. "I can stay with her a bit longer if you'd like. And I'll leave some fresh support bandages with your staff too."

"No, thank you. You've done enough, really. I'm sure you had appointments before I crashed your afternoon."

"I do have one other farm to visit." Tess checked her watch. "We'll send a bill over, if that's okay."

"Of course." Susannah enclosed Billie Jean into her comfortable stall and followed Tess out, hovering over her the whole time as Tess handed over a small box of elasticated bandages to one of the grooms.

"This really is a nice place you have here," Tess said when they made it back to her car. "I came here a couple of times when I was still a wee one."

"You did?"

"Easter Egg hunt, one time. Can't remember why else. There was a young man greeting all the visitors. I think that must have been your husband? James, was it?"

"Jimmy, yes. This was his family home, but he wanted to do more with it." Susannah gestured towards the stables. "So it's all down to me now. To usher in a new age of Midsummer. Which I'm sure you also didn't read about in the papers."

Tess tried to look like she never saw a word of it. "What sort of things? I overheard some chatter about an amusement park."

"Good lord, no." Susannah visibly shuddered. "There are some properties to renovate that people can rent for holidays, that sort of thing.

Maybe one day I could even turn it into a retreat for artists or something. But the sanctuary, that's my pet project. As it were."

"Horses?"

"And donkeys and dogs. All the animals that need space to stretch their legs. I have the room, so why not?"

"Huh."

"What?" Susannah demanded.

"I just didn't expect that from you, that's all. It's very...charitable."

"Well, you shouldn't believe everything you hear, Dr Robertson."

It was just reflex, but Tess stuck her hand out, now that it was free of the disposable gloves she used for treatment.

There was a frozen moment between them where Susannah looked down almost in confusion, but eventually she took the hint and extended her own hand for the briefest of shakes.

"I guess I'll be seeing you around," Tess said.

"It's a small village, so I suppose you will."

With that, Susannah turned on the firm heel of her riding boots, the tan leather moulded to her shapely calves, and started back towards the house.

Tess should have jumped straight in the car, but instead she watched every step of Susannah walking away until the path bent and took her out of sight.

Well, damn.

Chapter 8

IT TOOK THE REST OF the afternoon for Susannah to settle. She flitted from room to room, unable to focus on any particular task for more than a few minutes at a time. She made calls and left a lot of half-written emails in drafts, but whenever she got a chance, she checked in with the grooms to make sure Billie Jean wasn't in any more discomfort.

She paused for a moment to thank her lucky stars, or whatever it was a person thanked when they didn't really have religion, that a vet had been so close by. And so competent.

That, Susannah hadn't expected. She was aware her temper could lead her to rash decisions, but Tess, in all her workday calmness, had been the perfect woman for the job in the field.

Which didn't make Susannah's previous decision wrong, per se. She wasn't entirely convinced by the Elliotts' vet practice, pleasant though Margo and her husband were. It probably did show ambition that they'd brought someone in from London, but Tess was certainly not what that description immediately conjured to mind.

"I'm considering having you chipped," Finn said when they finally stumbled across Susannah back in her office. "No matter where I look for you today, you're not there."

"Well, I'm here now. Did you see Dave? He came out to help me with Billie Jean and the horse box."

"He said. Sent him back to get dinner on, didn't I? I've spent some time talking to your solicitor about Robin's article, and she has a legal strategy to discuss with you. Rather you than me—I just about dozed off making an appointment for it in your diary."

Finn sat in the visitor's chair in front of Susannah's glass-topped desk. "You've also got a spot to speak to the council planning committee next week, to start getting approval for all the changes around here."

"Why are you saying that like I've been invited to a funeral?" Susannah asked.

"Because I heard that Jonathan is already out there trying to whip up opposition. Robin might not have the standing to stop you herself, but it seems she's not above calling in a few favours over there. Or paying out a few backhanders." Finn fiddled with their glasses. "She thinks all she has to do is stop you for now, then keep trying to challenge your ownership of this place."

"Surely not everyone is susceptible to her bullying and bribery?" Susannah asked. "I know politics can be grubby, but there must be some decent people we can appeal to? I really don't want to go down the path of bribing or back-stabbing for my cause."

"She's hoping she can harass you, or maybe even, uh, shame you into handing it over. I tried getting something concrete out of Jonathan, since he's in the loop on everything, and he sort of implied that Robin would pay you off to get her hands on all this. To 'keep it in the family' as he put it."

"I guess that's what a few generations of total privilege will do for you," Susannah replied, sinking her head into her hands. It was a little surprising that Jonathan still spoke of the family so fondly, but he'd been working with Robin long enough that he probably was as good as family now. That was some consolation for him then, since he never got the commitment from Jimmy that he wanted. "She wants it, so she just assumes she'll get it. Remind me how I never developed that sense of sheer entitlement?"

Finn opened their mouth to say something in response, before quickly closing it. Maybe some things were better left unsaid between employer and employee.

Perhaps Susannah was losing perspective a little. Robin going full Marie Antoinette with the privilege certainly didn't erase the charmed existence that Susannah had been born and then married into.

"The horse is okay?" Finn tried instead.

"Yeah, but it's been a bit of a day, all told." Susannah sat up straight. "You know what would cheer me up?"

"Uh, cheering you up isn't technically in my job description?"

"Never mind that. I think you know what I want. You just have to say it out loud."

Finn hesitated. "Not the dungeon. Come on, Susannah. We have work to do."

"I've told you not to call it that. Come along. Let's take ourselves downstairs."

"But the solicitor! The council!"

Susannah was on her feet, her riding boots traded hours ago for soft leather slippers better for prowling the big old house. She yanked a hair band from around her wrist and pulled back her long blonde curls into a tidy ponytail.

"Just an hour. You'll work up an appetite for dinner, which means you'll appreciate Dave's cooking even more."

"You've been out riding half the day. Won't you just end up working all night when I go home?" Finn's resolve had weakened, and they were falling in step as Susannah led the way down the hall to the back stairs.

"That's my problem. We deserve this, trust me. There are weeks and months of trouble and hard work to come. We should relax while we can."

"There aren't many bosses like you," Finn said as they reached the door at the foot of the stairs.

The house had various basements and cellars—mostly around the kitchen for wine and other kinds of storage. This, though, was one of Susannah's favourite features in the whole mansion. The office was comfortable, and her bedroom was an oasis for sure. There was even the home gym up in a converted part of the attic space, in what would once have been servants' quarters. Susannah had reclaimed it when the last of the live-in staff had moved out.

"Okay, pick your poison." Susannah held up two DVD cases from the cabinet in the corner.

"I've memorized both of those by now."

"That's right, *Woman of the Year* it is. Great choice. Can't go wrong with a bit of Hepburn."

"Audrey?" Finn asked, more in hope than certainty.

"Katharine," Susannah corrected with a huff.

The projector screen fired up with the press of a button, and Susannah sank into the huge leather sofa that dominated the space, set at a perfect viewing distance. The lighting was low and warm, and there was a small fridge stocked with white wine and a selection of beers. It was what less enlightened people would call a man cave, even though there were no men in evidence. She pulled a bag of popcorn from the cabinet beside the couch.

"Is this the one where she's a hot journalist? Or the one with the tiger?" Finn took their preferred spot, tucked into the opposite corner of the large couch.

"You mean *leopard*, and yes she's a hot journalist. Her husband can't handle her workaholic ways, and they sort of accidentally adopt a kid and—"

Finn groaned into a cushion. "Okay yeah, I know which one this is. Mercy, please. Let's just watch it instead of you giving me the bullet points."

Susannah was lost to the world as soon as the opening credits rolled. She sighed in contentment and reached for the popcorn every so often as those signature Hepburn pantsuits dominated the screen.

Finn might have protested, but they were equally enthralled as they sipped at a bottle of beer. The surround sound brought all the detail to life beautifully, chasing away Susannah's remaining headache and the nagging thoughts about Robin and her schemes, or of Tess and how a flannel shirt really suited her.

Wait, what?

No, it was just because the Katharine Hepburn character shared a name with her. That had to be it. Damn that Tess Harding, bringing unbidden thoughts of Tess the vet right along with her.

"Distracted?" Finn asked, startling Susannah from her internal argument. "That's the first time you haven't said the lines right along with her."

"I could do just as well without you, you know." Susannah could say that because they both knew it wasn't true.

Before long, Finn's phone rang, and Susannah knew the fun part of her evening was officially over. She grabbed Finn's phone and answered for them. "I'm sending Finn home now, Dave! Sorry for working them so late." She hung up. "Go on, you. Get home to your lovely partner. I've got dinner waiting for me upstairs."

"You'd better get up there and eat something," Finn said, not for the first time. "Don't just stay down here all night telling yourself popcorn and wine is enough of a dinner."

"I'll be fine. There are plates made up in the fridge. I haven't starved yet." Susannah led Finn up to the front door.

"Maybe you could invite some friends up from the village sometimes. Host some movie nights," Finn suggested. "Shut up some of the gossip, and then I wouldn't break out into a cold sweat at the thought of watching Bette Davis in *Dark Victory* for the twentieth time."

"It's always going to be this way, Finn. As long as I'm in a mansion and people are worrying about having enough money for their winter fuel, they'd rather stay away and gossip about me. That's okay, it's part of the job. A few movie screenings won't do much to change that. Nor will going to yoga classes at the village rec centre, before you start nudging me about that again."

"It couldn't hurt. Oh, don't forget to fill out the retainer forms for the vet that I left on your desk. He was quite keen to get you all signed up so they can assign someone to cover the horses."

"Right. The man from the other day."

"Exactly. Unless you've changed your mind?"

"Night, Finn. Drive safe." Susannah closed the door and leaned back against it. She heaved out a sigh of something like relief, or maybe just frustration, and made her way to the kitchen. It wasn't worth the telling-off from Finn in the morning not to fish something out of the fridge now, before getting back to the film.

Her footsteps echoed a little despite the soft slippers, just quiet thuds that reminded Susannah how alone she was in this old pile of stone. Maybe it was time she looked for a dog of her own, not just ones she'd home in the sanctuary. A friendly fellow like Waffles could be just the trick.

Which was absolutely no excuse for Tess's face to swim unbidden across her thoughts again. Picking out some cold cuts and cheese, Susannah made an impromptu picnic to take back downstairs. She'd finish the movie and then go back to work, despite telling Finn she wouldn't. It all had to get done sometime.

She was woken by a gentle shake at her shoulder, opening her eyes to see grey light filtering in through half-opened curtains. Susannah was face down on her desk, some form or other stuck to her cheek, thanks to the charming fact of her having drooled a little in her sleep.

"Ow! Jesus!" Sitting up was her first mistake. Her bones and muscles had settled into the reality of her sleeping at a ninety-degree angle in her desk chair, and realigning them to a more human posture was painful indeed.

The hand on her shoulder was swiftly removed as Susannah stretched out her aches and pains, yawning heavily throughout. "You fell asleep at your desk," Finn said as though it wasn't obvious. "So much for it being wise for me to leave you alone."

Their voice was soothing, as always, the Scottish burr tempered by a faint rasp. There was just a slight tone of talking the crazy person down from the ledge that Susannah didn't entirely appreciate.

"You go and freshen up," Finn continued, urging Susannah with a light touch at her elbow. "You have one of the solicitors coming over this morning to talk about your defamation options, and you should probably look a little better than this."

Susannah looked down at her crumpled blouse, and swept a hand across her cheek only to find smudged mascara and what appeared to be cracker crumbs from her little feast. Her tongue felt like someone had carpeted it overnight, and the dull timpani beat across her forehead and both temples suggested that she hadn't stopped at a glass of wine with dinner. Drinking alone wasn't exactly a great habit to develop.

"I'll be in the shower," Susannah replied. "If you could summon up some breakfast with a massive pot of tea, there's a bonus in it for you."

"Getting ready to be your stand-in chef. Bacon sandwiches and a vat of Yorkshire's finest blend will be ready for you downstairs in twenty."

"Lifesaver."

Showering and getting dressed in record time, Susannah decided to leave make-up for after the restorative food and drink. With some paracetamol stashed in the pocket of her trousers, she jogged down to the smell of sizzling bacon and the sounds of a kitchen being properly used.

"Finn!" Susannah made sure her greeting was warm even though her head was still pounding. "Damn, that bacon smells good."

"You know, I do love cooking," Finn said. "Maybe I could do some of the catering instead of getting Joan to do it."

"Like I don't overwork you as it is. You do more than enough. I'd be lost without you."

"Well, I have some candidates for the personal chef position that I'll vet so you can interview the best of them."

"Thank you, Finn." Susannah poured herself tea from the pot that was steaming at the centre of the table. "I know there haven't been as many challenging events since it's been just me. It's taken a while to get everything back on track, but you're doing great. Did we try reaching out to Francine to see if she'll come back?"

"Hmm." Finn was definitely hiding something.

"Oh, go on, tell me."

"Francine may have had another offer," Finn said, fussing with the bacon and removing it from the heat. "One that she accepted, I believe. She started work already."

"Oh? If this is about money…" Susannah would prefer a familiar face, someone who already knew how she liked things. Breaking in a new person just sounded exhausting. "I know Jimmy was the one to hire her and that we entertained more when he was here, but that's all going to change now. She could run a little café for the holiday cabin guests."

"I'm not so sure that would work." Finn served up two perfect bacon sandwiches, and Susannah's stomach growled. "Since her loyalties seem to have shifted quite a bit."

"Oh, you're not telling me…"

"I'm afraid Robin is her new employer. Even if you offered more money, she seems to have bought into this fantasy that Robin is the rightful heir to Midsummer. God, this is all starting to sound like Shakespeare again."

"Why is that woman so obsessed with taking everything I have?" Susannah groaned the question more than she asked it. "It was bad enough she took Jonathan under her wing after he quit here. What next? Am I going to go down to the stables and find her riding Billie Jean?" She looked at her sandwiches, willing the fresh betrayal not to wilt her appetite. Nope, she still wanted to devour them. "No, we won't try to win her back. We'll find someone even better. Tell Jonathan next time you speak that this had better be the last I hear about Robin poaching my staff. My lawyers are already working on obliterating her, so she should really stop adding to that list."

"If you say so." Finn did their best to look upbeat about the prospect.

Handling all of Susannah's calls and vindictive relatives couldn't be an easy job. Maybe it was already time to look at raises again. "I do say so." Susannah took a hearty bite, just to show she wouldn't be disheartened in her own house. "Now, don't let me hold you up. I'm sure you have plenty to do that isn't running after me. I really appreciate the cooked breakfast, though."

Finn scurried off to tackle their to-do list.

Susannah sipped at her tea. How could good old loyal Francine seriously go to Robin? Why didn't any of the staff see Susannah as the rightful successor? Robin hadn't lived at Midsummer in twenty years, although most of the original staff would have been there then. Had the staff really known and disapproved of Susannah and Jimmy's arrangement for seeing other people of their preferred genders? Surely in that case they'd have been more likely to leave while Jimmy was still alive?

Which left two equally unappealing options: They'd all been promised something by Robin. Or they just didn't like Susannah and found her so unpleasant or unfair to work for that even leaving their jobs was worth it. That one was definitely worse but at least it felt a bit less likely than the first option. Who knew what lies had been spun, especially now that the veiled aspersions had made it even into the newspapers.

At the next opportunity, Susannah was going to let her have it with both barrels. That article had crossed the line, so nothing was off-limits now when it came to hitting back.

She just hoped that she wouldn't have to.

Chapter 9

"You!" Margo called out as she came into the pub to join Tess at a corner table. "Why are you hiding out in here?"

"I'm done for the day. My last appointment finished thirty minutes ago. Are you keeping track or something?"

"No, I wanted to give you a bloody big kiss!" And Margo did exactly that, laying a smacker right on Tess's cheek. "I don't know what you did the other day with that horse, but a certain someone has gone and changed her mind!"

"Sorry, what?" Tess set her half-empty pint back on the table, careful to place it right on the beer mat. "Who did what now?"

"Karlson. Midsummer Estate. She called about ten minutes ago and asked us to send over paperwork. She wants us as her main vet after all."

Tess rocked back against the cushioned bench, exhaling loudly in surprise. "Did she really?"

"Look at my face!" Margo pointed to her beaming smile. "Really! I thought her horse just had a sprain."

"Well, yeah. I just handled it, really. You know I started out as an equine specialist before the big city sucked me into domestic animals. I guess I'm not the incompetent numpty she took me for on my first day."

"Or maybe you flirted your way round her?" Margo waved to Adam, who was bringing over their soft drinks. "Wouldn't be the first time, Tess. You do have form when it comes to charming the ladies."

Tess took a smug little sip from her glass. "I'd hardly say that. And I'm sure there's nobody less interested in me than Lady Karlson. I'd be making a right fool of myself."

Babs shot them a suspicious glare from behind the bar at mention of her boss's name.

Tess realized their conversation had been getting a bit raucous, and it seemed people were loyal around these parts. All the more surprising when most people tended towards an "off with their heads" approach to the landed gentry. Tess smiled and steered the conversation back to details, making good progress on her pint. "So are we getting all her business?"

"Looks like it." Adam loosened his tie, then sipped at his bottled beer. "Bloody good job, T. You'll want the nod for her on-demand position, we're assuming?"

"Say what? Position?" Tess willed her brain not to wander down inappropriate paths. "Oh, you mean the go-to person up on the estate?"

"You won't have to work up there all the time—she doesn't have enough work for that yet," Margo replied. "But you'll be expected to put in an appearance most weeks for now. Think you can handle her?"

"Of course!" Tess said. "I mean, the horses. I can handle the horses. She's going to have rescue dogs too. I, uh, got a quick tour when I was up there seeing to Billie Jean."

Margo leaned across to smack Tess on the arm. "You kept that bit quiet! Well, whatever you did, it's amazing. Puts us on another level completely and means I can take a few months off to have this baby without worrying about us paying the bills. I knew you'd come through for me one way or another, mate."

"I was sort of coming through for myself as well," Tess said. "I have sunk everything I have into the practice. I'm just glad it's all working out, but she's a tricky one. I don't think we should treat it as a done deal yet, I mean. She could fire us next week for not putting ribbons in the horses' manes."

"Speak of the Devil." Adam nodded towards the bar.

Sure enough, Susannah had just appeared. She was in conversation with Babs and the young lanky lad who helped tend bar most evenings. Susannah looked a lot less stressed than the last time Tess had seen her, and the riding gear had been traded for a sharp black skirt suit that wouldn't look out of place on a lawyer or a banker.

"I'm sure she's not here for us if she just called you." Tess debated whether to go up and get another drink. She didn't want it to look like

Susannah's presence had drawn her over there. Though would that be the worst thing?

There was something interesting about the woman, no denying that. Something about her kept tugging on Tess's imagination, but she couldn't be sure whether it was the glimpses of a regular person she saw behind the fancy title or the way Susannah had seemed transformed while worrying over her beloved horse. Whatever it was, Tess knew that there was more going on in there than her superficial first impressions had allowed for.

Besides, it wasn't as if they were likely to become friends. This was an honest-to-god lady, a landowner and firmly a social class or two above Tess. Susannah Karlson was not going to be in the market for working-class veterinarians who probably thought the aristocracy should be abolished, other than to medicate her horses and neuter her rescue dogs.

Dave suddenly wandered into the pub, smiling at someone Tess assumed was Finn. They both made a beeline for Tess's table.

"Finn," Adam said with a welcoming smile, confirming Tess's theory. "Haven't seen you for ages, not since I came out to Dave's ewes last time. Have you met our new colleague, Tess?"

"I've heard of her." Finn shot a sympathetic smile at Tess that said it was probably not all that positive. "Well, that you're a fan of my kitchen, anyway."

"It's amazing," Tess replied. "Is that the paperwork you need from us?"

"Yup, here's the new contract." Finn slid it across the table.

"Thanks for that. How are the sheep, Dave?" Adam asked. "You had Tess out the other day, didn't you?"

"Yes, all good," Dave replied and glanced at Tess. "Thank you for that. I heard the horse is doing better. Lucky you were there."

Tess shrugged. "I just go where I'm needed. Thanks for the assist with Billie Jean. It's nice to meet you, Finn. I'm glad you haven't had to call me back out for the horse. She responded well to my treatment."

"Susannah seems happy," Finn replied. "Which is a bit of a miracle this week. Guess that's why you got the gig. You all okay for drinks?"

Adam and Margo nodded, having barely started on theirs.

Tess didn't know if she was supposed to accept the offer. Why were all these social things so bloody fraught? She lifted her almost empty glass. "Well, I'm on the bitter so…"

"I'll get that," Susannah said, moving from the front of the bar to come and join them. "I see the whole practice is up to speed on new developments, then?"

"We are, yes," Margo answered. "And thank you for reconsidering. We won't let you down."

"So, who do I get as my go-to, then?"

"Is that what you're calling it?" Tess couldn't help but respond.

"Well, the deal is I have a point person. A specialist who puts me and my animals first, day or night. Who's the lucky winner? Elliot, Elliot, or Robertson?" Susannah turned and motioned to Babs, who handed her a freshly poured pint of best.

She set it down in front of Tess, who was treated to an unavoidable glimpse down Susannah's blood-red silk blouse, which seemed barely buttoned from this angle.

Tess focused on Susannah's elegant necklace for a moment, hoping it might look as though that had caught her attention.

The smirk on Susannah's face as she straightened confirmed she had seen right through that little ploy.

"We were just discussing that," Adam answered for her. "And since she already has a rapport with Bobby—"

"Billie Jean," Tess and Susannah corrected him as one.

"Right, there you go. So, yes, you get Dr Robertson. Now that you've seen firsthand how brilliant she is, I'm sure you know you're in good hands."

Tess felt her face heat up as she took the first taste of her new ale.

"Yes, I think I might be," Susannah replied. "Still, Finn here can run you through the contract before they're quite done for the day. I, on the other hand, have places to be."

"Sure thing." Finn took a seat as soon as Susannah swept out, while Dave went off to order their drinks. "Are you all ready to be bored? You'll need your solicitor to go over all this anyway."

"We have time," Margo said. "Let's go through it."

In all the excitement over landing a new client, Tess forgot all about her new flat until the estate agent rang to ask when she'd be picking up the keys. Finally, a chance to unpack properly and start settling in.

Any residual fear that coming so close to home would send her running in a blind panic seemed to have completely faded now. Hayleith felt both familiar and just strange enough to be the right place for Tess at just the right time.

There weren't a ton of properties to choose from in a town this small, so she was pleased that her choice was in a quiet lane that ran down the back of the pub, just far enough that any noise from the beer garden wouldn't travel and disturb her on quiet nights in.

Tess brought Margo to see it with her after she'd picked up the keys. It was silly not to want to go in alone for the first time, but the most reliable thing in the world was Margo's unbridled curiosity. Some would call it nosiness, but Tess was much too good a friend for that.

"Wow!" Margo said, looking around at the impressive space.

"This is nicer than I thought," Tess said. The walls were bare and white, the ceilings high, and the windows let in a ton of natural light. A person could paint in a space like this. Shame Tess had the artistic ability of a drunk pelican. "You never know quite what to expect, no matter how many pictures are on the website."

"I was sure it couldn't be too bad. A nice young family had the place last time I knew the tenants. It's such great timing that it came up now, although you'd be very welcome to stay with us as long as you want."

"Nah." Tess waved off the idea as they traipsed through to the kitchen. She wasn't a bad cook, and there was actually space to move around, which was a bonus. "I know you're itching to start on your nursery at home, and my room is the obvious choice."

Margo blushed, utterly caught. "Still, we have a few months yet."

"It's time I had my own space. I've gone from home to uni dorms to flat-shares to living with one girlfriend and then Caroline. I don't think I've ever had a house to myself for more than a week."

"Then I hope you'll be very happy here. Two bedrooms, right?"

"Yeah, one for me and one for Waffles. At least around here, people rent to you if you have pets."

Margo was already off up the stairs, unable to contain herself. Tess followed, pleased that the stairs didn't creak. Cursory inspections of the bathroom and the smaller bedroom confirmed all was well, and she hurried to join Margo in the master bedroom.

It took up half of the top floor on its own, with a full wall of windows. Tess actually spun around on the spot, completely taken with it.

"So this is where the magic will happen, eh?" Margo says. "Sorry, is it weird when I tease you about this, given the whole...you know...uni thing? I promise I really am cool with everything."

"Honestly, Margo, I don't even think about...you know. It's ancient history, and we're both living our best lives now—just about."

It had been a while since Margo had brought up their ill-fated one-night stand during the last year of university. Tess had never asked if Adam knew—if that was the root of his unfunny jokes about threesomes. It wasn't her business, and it wasn't relevant to where they were now.

"You're such a good friend," Margo said, and she was actually getting a bit weepy. She had cried exactly three times in all the years Tess had known her, so for a moment Tess had no idea what to do.

"Fucking hormones, sorry," Margo said.

Tess gave her a quick hug. "It's just your mum superpowers starting to activate, don't worry."

"I know, I know. Who actually owns this place, by the way? Is it one of the people who lived here, then moved away?"

Tess skimmed through her emails to see if it was mentioned. She stood by the window that overlooked the quiet courtyard shared with three other town houses like this, the little brook that ran between it, and the beer garden of the pub. Tess didn't think she'd ever get to like its name: The Spiky Thistle. *Where am I? Right. Emails about the house.*

"It's actually all signed with the estate agent." Tess got to the email with the copy of her lease. "Wait, this will have the owner's name on it somewhere."

And sure enough, right above Tess's name and the company acting as agents, there was the one person she really should have expected at this rate. Tess groaned.

"What?" Margo asked. "Oh wait. It's not...?"

"Got it in one," Tess said. "Our biggest client is also technically my landlord. Why exactly did I move back up here again? This kind of thing wouldn't happen in London."

"It'll be fine. You have a contract, you have rights. And Lady Muck seems to be almost tolerant of you these days. That has to count for something, right?"

"I hope so," Tess said. "Come on, we should get back to work."

Chapter 10

JOAN ARRIVED EARLY, WHICH WAS quite unlike her, and brought the most beautiful spread that Susannah had ever seen outside of a five-star restaurant. Before she could say a word, dishes were being loaded into the giant fridge, with a list of instructions taped to the door for later.

"Hey Boss?"

Susannah froze as she heard Babs call out from the kitchen door.

"Oh," Joan said sharply as Babs reversed into the room, carrying a wooden crate full of gently clinking bottles. "It's you."

Susannah supposed she should be glad her drinks order wasn't dropped on the floor out of spite. No one needed that much broken glass this early in the day. Babs was supposed to have been bringing the wine more than an hour from now. This was going to look like meddling. "All okay here?" Susannah asked. "Bit of a scheduling overlap, but we're all professionals aren't we?"

"Morning!" Jonathan said, entering through the side door as though he'd never stopped working here. Great, just the absolute last interloper she needed. Was he here to spy? Deliver more irritating news? Susannah had to bite her tongue not to bark at him. Dressed in muted tartan trousers with a matching waistcoat over a black shirt, he looked both fashionable and stuffy. "Just wanted a quick word about today?"

"Well, I've left you everything you need," Joan addressed Susannah and shoved the last few platters into the fridge. "Just needs someone who can operate an oven and handle the warm plates. It's all in the instructions."

"I can settle up with you now?" Susannah offered. She fired off a quick text to Finn, summoning them for crowd control, if nothing else.

"I'll send the bill," Joan said. "No particular rush, thank you."

"Turned the café into a Michelin-starred bistro, then, have you?" Babs asked as she unloaded the bottles much slower than necessary.

"And what business is that of yours?" Joan began moving towards the door, but that put her on a collision course with Jonathan.

"Let's keep things civilised, please, ladies," Jonathan said with a heavy sigh. "Nobody wants a repeat of the Halloween party, do they?"

"Picked up psychic abilities along with that haircut, have you?" Joan asked.

That was enough to set Babs off, and she was marching across the kitchen in her leopard print blouse and black skirt to put herself between Jonathan and Joan. "That is no way to talk to him."

"I'll speak to that boy any way I damn well please," Joan said. "He's the one who quit on me and Susannah to go and work for Robin Karlson."

"As he's entitled to do," Babs corrected. "For someone who's always telling people how to change their businesses, you certainly don't like any disruption in your own little world."

"Honestly, it's fine," Susannah tried to intervene, but she was used to being summarily ignored when these two crossed paths.

"I happen to believe in loyalty," Joan said, drawing herself up to her full height in her flowing blue maxi dress. "Now he's probably here to cause some trouble, aren't you, boy?"

"No," Jonathan replied. "But I did just want to mention that you'll need a vegan option for Councillor Javit today. Oh, and he's bringing Robin as his guest. You did give everyone a plus one for the presentation and drinks."

Finn arrived then, and Susannah saw her opportunity to escape. Cursing as she scurried upstairs to change, she felt a smidgen of guilt at leaving Finn to wrangle with the civil war in her kitchen. If Robin wanted to throw Susannah off her game today, she'd have to do a lot better than crashing the canapés and small talk.

Small talk might have been the most excruciating part of it all, worse even than how Susannah's new high heels pinched terribly at the toes. She made sure that every glass was filled and that the village teens were passing around trays of canapés without insulting anyone. She couldn't remember quite which two these were, but Finn kept track of all that.

"This is a lovely glass of red," Councillor Johnson was saying, snapping Susannah back to attention. "You're really spoiling us today."

"Oh, this? Well, I like to get my best cooks and sommeliers on the case when I have important guests." Listening to herself, Susannah was glad she didn't have much of a gag reflex.

"It really is a pleasure, Lady Karlson. I've heard great things about your entertaining here at Midsummer. I, for one, was glad to make the list."

Susannah gave her best encouraging smile. "It's overdue, I know. I haven't felt very festive for most of the year since Jimmy passed, but he would be the first to tell me to pick myself up and get on with things here." The small lie that her own vision had in fact been Jimmy's still felt unpleasant on her tongue. "And I thought, who better to show its potential to? These plans are all about community."

"Community?" Councillor Javit interrupted without a second thought. "Which part of the community will be spending hundreds of pounds renting out a holiday cabin for a stag weekend that ends up trashing half the village?"

"Oh dear. It seems you've been given some inaccurate information there, Councillor," Susannah replied without gritting her teeth, though it was a close call. "Have you had a chance to look at the brochure?" There was a small stack of them on every surface. No excuse for not doing the homework, but leave it to politicians to not even do the bare minimum.

"No, but I have my sources," Councillor Javit said. "Forgive me if I trust the word of a dear friend over the new face in town."

"New face...I've lived here for almost ten years!" Susannah felt the indignation creeping in and tried to wrestle back control of it. "Still, that feeling of something new can be so good for the local economy."

"And where was it you studied economics?" Robin glided into the little cluster of visitors as though she had wheels under her plain brown brogues. Jonathan hovered by her elbow as always. "Only I happened to study it at St. Andrew's, as you know. As we always say, if it's good enough for royalty, it must be a decent wee school."

There was polite laughter to greet her, a flurry of handshakes, and air kisses, all of which seriously interfered with Susannah's opportunity to yank the bitter cow out of there by the prissy bun in her hair. The thing probably detached anyway, as lifeless as everything else about her.

"Robin! I understand you came as Councillor Javit's guest," Susannah said, eyes narrowing. "I thought you'd be much too busy for a little event like this, or I would have called you direct."

"I am, as you all know, very invested in the future of Midsummer. As with so many things around here, I'm also a part of its past and its present, when I'm allowed to be. My brother was a good man, and his focus was always on continuing the wonderful traditions our family has built here. Even before he was made a member of the House of Lords, James put so much work into this place."

"Lord Karlson is greatly missed, Robin," Councillor Johnson replied. "Though he always said his dear lady wife here did so much in running the estate. Couldn't do it without her."

Susannah bestowed her most grateful smile on him.

"No doubt, no doubt," Robin replied, pretending to really consider it. "But as I'm sure you all know, gentlemen, a good wife needs a very particular skillset. But not every woman is capable of leading in the same way as men are. Now, I was raised to lead because our late father saw great things ahead for James and me both."

It set Susannah's teeth on edge, all this James nonsense. No one, not even his own mother, had ever called him anything but Jimmy. It felt like they were talking about some stranger, and Susannah hated it. She stepped up, grabbing her sister-in-law by the elbow so no one could see, and made sure the grip pinched. "I do believe if you watch the presentation with everyone else, Robin, you'll see that leadership is very much in my skillset. But since you've been such a help with that, I just wanted to run a few last-minute questions past you. In *private*."

Susannah was relieved when Robin let herself be steered rather than making a scene. They ducked into one of the empty rooms along the hall, the one with the billiards table that no one ever played on. Even when Jimmy was alive, he'd only come in there to read, not to knock some balls around with a stick.

"How dare you crash this event!" Susannah asked as soon as the door was closed. "What is this, Robin? What have I ever done to you? First the papers, now you're sabotaging me in person? You could at least fight fair. That's what I've been doing."

"I'm fighting to win. You're going to turn this beautiful place into a theme park, some gaudy American mess with a Ferris wheel and delinquents selling drugs in the bathrooms. I won't stand for it."

"It's going to have a few distant holiday cabins that will help fund a horse sanctuary. Where are you getting these crazy ideas?"

"Oh, I know what you're really up to," Robin hissed. "You've always wanted to push this place into something James didn't want. The sun, moon, and stars had to be arranged to suit Susannah. Every business decision, every purchase, every sale… He stopped listening to me. We used to be such a team!"

"We were married, Robin. Sometimes things shift that way. I know he still respected your opinion. He said all the time 'Robin would do this' or 'Robin says that'. We were never excluding you. Jimmy said you'd be glad to be rid of all the responsibility for once."

"His name is *James*," Robin said. "But by all means, you go out there and make a fool of yourself. Show them your vague pictures and your idiotic plans. They know you're not qualified for this; you're just a meaningless title from a bankrupt estate. I've already lined up enough votes to get your planning permission refused, so good luck ever turning them back."

"I will," Susannah replied. "But I shouldn't have to. Can't we just get along, Robin?"

"No." Robin fixed her jacket and pushed past Susannah to open the door. "He regretted marrying you, did you know that? Said so in the hospital. That with a bit more daring he could have lived quite openly, but you talked him into all the cloak and dagger routine to get your hands on his money."

"What?" Susannah reeled back as though Robin had struck her. The idea for their marriage had never come from Susannah, and more than once when Jimmy's head had been turned by a new lover, she'd checked in with him, told him she'd be amenable to an amicable divorce if he ever needed it.

Not once, not for a second, had she ever considered Jimmy might resent her. They had both agreed, over and over, that pursuing same-sex relationships would be ruinous for both of them, outside of discreet and sanctioned affairs. She'd been so desperate for security and stability after wriggling out of her own family's clutches that maybe she hadn't questioned their plan enough. The very thought that Jimmy had felt trapped by that in the end, that she'd somehow boxed him into a life of regrets, was the straw that broke the camel of lingering politeness's back.

"Get. Out."

"This is my family. Get out before I drag you out. And I wrangle horses daily, so make no mistake, pulling you across the hall by your hair will barely be a workout for me. Get the *fuck* out of my house, and don't you darken my doorstep again, plus one or otherwise."

Robin looked like she might argue the toss, but whatever Susannah's furious expression had settled into apparently gave her second thoughts. The door slammed, and Susannah stood there staring at it.

Surely Robin had made that up to hurt her? But she sounded so sure, so utterly convinced that it happened. If it had, was that justification for why she was trying so hard to wrest back control? Or was she just bitter and deluded, trying to tear strips off Susannah in any way she could?

She still hadn't decided by the time she stood up in front of the small gathering to make her presentation. Susannah's stomach roiled with anxiety. At first it felt as though the foundations of her world and much of her self-confidence had started to crumble beneath her. With a reassuring look from Finn, Susannah found her footing a few slides in and delivered the presentation as she'd intended. The room responded with polite applause.

"Thank you, Councillor Javit," she said as the man came over to shake her hand. She noticed Jonathan slipping out after checking his phone, no doubt summoned by Robin. He could report back how well it had gone. "If it's not too impolite, might I ask how you're planning to vote when my application comes up?"

"Ah." He looked at his shoes. "Please know, Lady Karlson, that it's nothing personal. I just have to go with what has the right *tone* for the area. You understand."

"I do." Susannah scanned the room, not seeing potential allies anymore. They were all Robin's people, it seemed, braying and slapping each other on the back as they drank her booze and made plans to deny her the business dream she'd always wanted. It was enough to make her want to scream, but of course that would never do. Susannah came from a long line of women who'd had to bite their tongues and outsmart men to get their way.

The prickling tears took Susannah by surprise, and she slipped out of the room as fast as her legs would carry her, hampered only by her damned high heels. At a loss for somewhere no one would come looking for her, she followed her feet in the direction of the stables.

Maybe that was for the best. Humans might keep letting her down, but the horses wouldn't.

The tears fell as Susannah walked, but at least there was no one around to witness them.

Chapter 11

This wasn't an official visit by any means, nor was it even strictly necessary. Billie Jean's first check-up had revealed the sprain to be healing nicely, and the lovely old girl had already been out for some light trotting around the paddock with the grooms.

Tess just happened to be in the area. Which wasn't hard when the Midsummer Estate comprised most of the area.

So what was a fifteen-minute detour when everything was just a drive away? Tess could call it excellent customer service for a new client that they really wanted to keep sweet. Tess was simply following through on her promise to herself to further her career to its maximum potential.

Yeah. Not exactly convincing.

She was already at the stables, and noticing a lack of activity. None of the estate staff seemed to be in evidence. Tess heaved a sigh of relief. At least this way no one would question her unscheduled visit.

She called out to Billie Jean on her way in, scuffing her wellies against the rough cement floor and kicking a few strands of hay with every step. Even though the stables were immaculate in every way, there was simply no containing hay to neat bales for each stall. Like glitter, some always got loose and found a way into every crack and crevice.

"Hey, girl." Tess patted the horse on her smooth nose. She got a whinny in response. It was only when Tess set her bag on the ground that she heard the snuffling sound. That was no horse. "You're looking good there, Billie Jean. Quiet in here today."

Nothing. Whoever made the sound had gone completely silent now. Maybe frozen in fear.

"I'm coming into the stall now," Tess said in her most "soothe the savage beast" tone. "Let's take one more look at that fine leg of yours."

The stall door swung outwards, the hinges perfectly oiled so there was barely a sound. Tess counted to three before stepping inside, Billie Jean swishing her tail and ignoring her all the while.

"You found me."

Tess wished she was more surprised to see Susannah sitting on the groomer's stool with her head in her hands. The clothes were especially fancy, a dress with one of those tiny jackets over the top and shoes with heels that could easily stab a person. Not that practical for strutting around the stables.

"I wasn't looking," Tess said. "I really did just come to check on Billie Jean here. I can go—"

"No, no," Susannah wiped her face with delicate fingers, sporting a manicure on her short, neatly kept nails. "You've already seen the worst of it, so we may as well just get through the awkward part."

"I'm sorry to intrude, really. Not the intruding type, as a rule."

"Apart from when you're trespassing, of course."

"Right. Apart from that. Again, not intentional," Tess said, just to correct the record. "Must have been another one of my wrong turns. Happens to the best of us. Just like having a cry in private."

Susannah smirked. Her mascara had run a little. It gave her that air of a tragic heroine. Her hair had been pinned up at some earlier point, but blonde strands had come loose all over the place. "Artfully mussed" looked annoyingly good on her.

"Is it anything you need help with? If you were worrying about your horse, she really is fine."

"How would you know? You just got here," Susannah wrapped her arms around herself. "Unless she was fine when you checked up on her the other day. Which rather begs the question of what you're doing here now?"

"Just being overcautious. First official patient and all that."

"Or did you think she was healing too quickly? Hmm? Maybe if you just eased off a bit, she'd show some more symptoms and you could prove your value a second time?"

Tess actually took a step back at that. "If you think for one minute I'd hurt an animal, that I'd prolong her pain by one second…just to… That's horrible. I can't believe you'd accuse anyone of something like that, let alone me, when I've done nothing to deserve it."

There was a sort of thundering in her ears. Tess couldn't remember the last time she was so angry.

"Oh, come on. I wasn't insulting your character or anything—"

"No, you were. That's exactly what you were doing." Tess wasn't on the back foot now. She marched down the side of the stall until she got right in Susannah's face. Her very shocked face. "You think because you sit up there with your money and your land that everyone else must be out to... what? Rob you? That we're all just peasants and criminals here to sully your lovely existence?"

"Now that's a little melodramatic. I thought you were only too pleased to be part of the staff around here."

There was that condescending tone again, that posh little scoff. It didn't even matter that Tess knew Susannah was born to all this, that she probably couldn't help her default position of looking down on everyone around her. Part of Tess felt very sure that if Susannah would just try, she might even pass for a normal human being.

"I might not have a title or two to my name, but I'm not going to stand here and be disrespected. I worked hard to get where I am. I studied and I put in the hours, and I went to a top university. I built a vet practice in London out of almost nothing, and even when it was practically stolen away from me, I still managed to work my way into starting fresh up here. I provide a service—one you need, by the way—and I charge a fair rate for it. That doesn't make me your staff, or your servant, or anything of the kind."

"Hey, hey!" Susannah raised her hands in surrender. "I was... Well, I'd say I was joking but that's not quite right. Oh, stop glaring at me like that. You're quite fearsome when you lose your temper, Miss Robinson."

"*Doctor* Robinson."

"And here you were telling me off about how titles don't matter."

Tess glared. She was still too mad to concede the point.

"I had a bad afternoon, okay?" Susannah said. "Caused by people being their worst selves all over the place. Greedy, selfish, destructive. So I got myself into a bit of a state after it all and came out here to get some good company and peace until they all left. Which you just interrupted with that perfect timing of yours."

"I'd prefer an actual apology." Tess folded her arms over her zipped-up padded jacket. "If you know how, that is."

"Oh, would you? And I'd like the council to stop denying me planning permission because they're all in the pocket of my sister-in-law, but we can't have everything."

"Can't we?"

"No. Are you really ready to fall out with me and cancel this contract before it's even come into force?" Susannah stood up then, getting in Tess's face. "Do you really want to go back to Margo and Adam and tell them you blew it? Again?"

"You'd like that, wouldn't you? Get someone else to do your dirty work for you? Well, I won't quit, so you're going to have to get your hands sullied this time and fire me."

"Oh, don't be stupid. Why would I fire you?" Susannah threw her hands into the air and turned away. "You're one of the few things around here that I don't hate."

Tess felt like she had just run into a plate-glass window she didn't know was there. "Oh, so now you're joking?"

"What?"

"You're still trying to be funny? Because you have been nothing but rude to me since I got here. Even when I was fixing up your horse. Even just now when I was asking if you were okay!"

Susannah turned back to face the fight. "Fine! I'm sorry! Actually, properly sorry. I'm so used to being on the defensive, especially lately. It seeps into every word and every thought, and suddenly everything comes out in raging bitch."

"Wow. That was some apology." Tess risked reaching out to pat Susannah on the arm. "I wasn't blaming you for everything that's wrong in the world, but I guess I got my answer on whether you're okay or not."

"Crying in a horse's stall really does provide its own answer on that one. Would you rather we took this up to the house? The clear-up should be done. I'm assuming you don't have anything on this evening if you're coming up here this late in the day?"

Tess wasn't quite sure how she got from a rage fit to a drinks invitation, so she took a moment to pat the horse's back, shamelessly playing for time. "I'm sorry too. For my tone, although some of the content still stands."

"Sounds like a truce to me. Besides, we need to get along, if for no other reason than my horses like you." She glanced at her favourite. "You're a damn traitor, Billie Jean."

That got a snort from the horse.

They stepped out of the stall, and Susannah closed the heavy wooden door behind them.

"These are some fantastic stables," Tess said. "When are you due to bring in more horses?"

"Going to look at a few in the next couple of weeks and take in as many as I can before I have to expand the facilities."

"I'm guessing that's what today was about? If you're that upset?"

"Yes, I'm afraid so," Susannah said as they made their way up the path to the house. Only Tess's Land Rover was still parked in the drive. "It looks like we have the place to ourselves, at least."

Instead of the grand front entrance, she led them around back to the kitchen door. There were signs of stacked trays and crates in the corners, no doubt tidied away after whatever event had been going on. It looked more like a restaurant kitchen than anything that belonged in a family home. A dishwasher hummed in the background.

"Shall we just sit ourselves in here?" Tess asked, nervous about going any further into the house. Her heart rate had returned to normal since her outburst, but she wasn't entirely confident in how settled things were between them. "Saves me intruding on your private quarters."

Well, that didn't come out quite right. They both audibly suppressed a snicker.

"You can intrude on my wine stash instead. I'm sure there's some left after the gathering. Unless you'd prefer a beer?"

"I do know a little about wine, you know." Tess took a seat on one of the high white stools that lined the kitchen island, a great big slab of chrome. It was definitely not a kitchen from a stuffy, old period drama, and that made her curious about the rest of the house. "But if you had something you think I'd like in the ale department..."

"Hmm." Susannah considered her for a moment. "Wait here." She disappeared out of the kitchen, leaving Tess to consider the scale of it. The rest of the house certainly looked big from the outside, but it must be downright massive. Ten, maybe fourteen bedrooms. It was the kind of stately home people rented out to get married in. Except for how there were people living in it.

"Did you get lost?" Tess couldn't help teasing when Susannah returned. It always seemed to deflate the tension between them. "Although I can see why you'd need a map even if you live here."

"It's not that big, really. Well, relatively, yes. You just...get used to it, I suppose. Here." Susannah handed over a bottle with a handwritten label.

"What's this?"

"Something locally brewed. Jimmy used to find the most ridiculous brews all over the place. I haven't really had cause to dip into them lately."

"Oh, if this is something special, I couldn't—"

"Please. It makes me happy to know someone will drink them. I try to push them off on Dave, but he's a Pilsner man. Whatever that means."

"I think it's like being a shiraz person, or something like that." Tess fished for her keys and pulled the bottle opener free. "I come prepared."

"In the Brownies, were you?"

"Yeah, and...?" Tess puffed out her chest. "Brownies, Guides, Rangers, and I was a Leader for a while."

"Were you really?" Susannah cocked an eyebrow. "You forgot about the Rainbows, by the way. Did you skip that stage?"

"Nope, they didn't have those when I was the right age." Tess sipped the ale. It was slightly creamy, heavy on the sediment as it dragged across her tongue. Very nice indeed. "What makes you think I'm not the type?"

"Oh no, you are. With your outdoors gear and all those practical skills. Did they have a junior vet badge then?"

"No."

"Someone told me once it's harder to get into a veterinary medicine degree here than it is for human medicine. Is that really true?"

Tess nodded. "It certainly used to be. Same for dentistry, I think. Something about fewer universities offering courses. It drives up competition. I was so lucky to get into Glasgow."

"I bet luck had nothing to do with it."

"Did you...?" Tess stopped.

"Study anything worthwhile? God no. I scraped my BA in History from Durham, but they were glad to see the back of me. I do think sometimes about trying to learn something more seriously. I'd rather listen to the experts on most subjects. Business, though? I've paid my dues there. That's all on instinct, and I learned on the job." Susannah swirled the ice in her glass. Something clear.

"Didn't feel like an ale, then?" Tess asked.

"Can't stand the stuff. Nothing a splash of vodka can't cure, though, so I went with a classic."

Tess had another sip and let the silence settle between them. It was almost comfortable, tucked away from the rest of the world like this. "Are you sure you're okay?" she asked just as they had lulled themselves into a sort of calm.

"Just the usual. Old straight white men trying to stand in my way. Apparently it's not what you do, but who you know around here."

Tess couldn't hold back a snort.

"Okay," Susannah continued. "I have a certain amount of privilege of my own, but seriously. I want to give people jobs. I want to give some animals a nice gentle retirement. And I don't want to be stuck in this giant doll's house with nothing meaningful to do. Is that so awful?"

"No, that's not awful at all."

"You know, when you're not shouting at me, you're actually quite a nice person, Tess."

"I'm starting to warm up to you, Susannah." Tess dragged the name out like they were making playground taunts. "And here I was worried I wouldn't make any new friends when I moved here."

"Right." Susannah downed her drink in one. "Who couldn't do with more friends?"

Chapter 12

Susannah surprised herself by almost bounding out of bed in the morning. Usually after a huge crying session and a few drinks she'd have been dreading the sunshine, but the Scottish weather had gifted a cool grey day to ease her in.

It helped, of course, that Tess didn't stay too late, and they didn't drink all that much in the end. Even better—probably those doctorly instincts at play—Tess had insisted they both drank plenty of water and reminded Susannah to set out a couple of painkillers by the bed, just in case. It all added up to enough energy for a session on the cross trainer and a spot of yoga to start the day.

Hopping into the shower, one of her favourite modernised parts of the house, Susannah emptied her mind as the cascade of water splashed down on her. It was cleansing and massaging in one, and some days she never wanted to get out from under the spray.

Her mind finally zoned back in on some detail or other, and that set her thinking about Tess and how reluctantly she'd made her excuses last night. Of course, Waffles had needed to be walked, and he'd been with Margo since lunchtime, but even so, Tess had been slow to actually get out the door.

Susannah leaned into the flow of water. When exactly was the last time someone had seemed to genuinely want to be in her company? Especially this past year when she'd been wrapped up in grief and stress—even less approachable than usual.

"Someone got a good night's sleep!" Finn declared as Susannah walked into the office, dressed in her one of her smartest suits, a navy pinstripe that always made her feel like she should be making bankers or politicians weep. She should have gone with it for the presentation yesterday.

"You look like a whole new woman," Finn said.

"Let's not overdo it."

"You disappeared before the end of the reception yesterday, and nobody had seen you by the time Dave came to pick me up. Is that good news, or…?"

"Alas, Finn, it seems a certain someone has been trying to use her name and connections to turn the council to her side. It's been quite successful too."

Finn slapped the desk in annoyance. With Finn's contact lenses swapped in for glasses, and a light sweater instead of the usual sharp tailoring, they looked softer today, more casual. It was quite appealing, really.

"So, what do we do?"

"Yesterday my answer was cry, get drunk, maybe go out after dark and shout obscenities at the moon."

"Did it work?"

"I changed the plan a little, which left me refreshed and ready enough to realise that it's time for a real charm offensive. Robin has sold these smarmy bastards a mirage. She has no power here, and doesn't make any decisions. Sure, she has money, but she's not the real carrier of the Karlson name anymore."

Finn leaned forward in their seat, sensing blood in the water. "And?"

"And we need to make everyone aware of that. Remind them who will be making the money and the deals around here. Who will be calling the shots. It's a new day, and it's time I stood up for myself properly. First stop: get a journalist from that local rag up here today. Time for more than just tossing a press release to the wind and hoping for the best."

"Really? A journalist?"

"Yes. I want all this reframed on the grieving widow. I'm not happy with my marriage being dismissed, because whatever our reasons for marrying, we were partners for years and kept all this going together. That doesn't mean it takes second place to some sibling nonsense. No, it has to be about me, about women succeeding, and how dare anyone get in the way."

Finn nodded and started tapping furiously on their tablet.

"Then I want to make appointments to go and see these horses that need to be stabled. Can you, uh...make sure someone from the vet surgery is free to come and check them with me?"

"No problem," Finn replied. "Anything else?"

Susannah hesitated again, digging the heel of her shoe into the thick carpet. It was a half-baked notion at best, an idea that mostly came to her in a dream. An idea that had persisted through exercise, a long shower, and dressing.

"Speaking of getting back on the horse, well, sort of... I don't suppose there are any little soirées coming up where I might cross paths with some interesting people? Only I think I've been stuck indoors as the grieving widow long enough, don't you?"

Finn actually squealed.

Should have seen that one coming.

"Are you serious? Oh, Susannah, that is such good news. That's progress is what that is!"

Fiddling with the button on her white blouse, Susannah avoided looking up for the moment. These things were excruciating enough to say without having to maintain eye contact.

"Yes, well. I admit I've been a little lonely up here. You've been wonderful, above and beyond, really. It's just I rather feel there might be at least someone interesting out there. Someone I could talk to about things other than work, and the inner workings of this place."

"You can—"

"I know, Finn. But you know what I mean. What you have with Dave in all his loveliness, I'd like to have that too—or at least see who's out there, just in case they turn out to be amazing."

Finn got up and walked slowly around the table, drawing Susannah into a sudden and fierce hug. They stood like that for a moment.

"Jimmy told me to move on when he left," Susannah said. "And, you know, I saw a woman or two in private now and then."

"So, no dating apps, then?" Finn asked. "You want to meet someone the old-fashioned way?"

Susannah nodded. "I don't really want my dating profile to end up in the papers, just to have a fun drink with someone, you know?"

"Oh, I certainly do know. Susannah, you don't have someone in mind already, do you?"

Damn that Finn and their suspicious mind. Honestly, Police Scotland didn't know what a top-class detective they were missing out on.

"Please, with the dating pool around here? I know you don't have to live in the big city to find your fellow queers these days, but if I wanted to meet a like-minded person, someone who probably won't rob me after the third date...any suggestions?"

"I'm afraid lesbian bars are a dying breed these days," Finn said. "But there are plenty of mixed places, and lots of one-off nights in great venues. I could come with you, you know, for moral support."

"Then I'd look like I was already coupled up."

"Ah, then a group? No? Wow, you're brave to face these places alone. I never could."

"If you think of anything, put it in my calendar? We have more important things to crack on with than my love life."

"How could anything be more important? You're ready to get back in the saddle, and I don't mean the one on Billie Jean. This is a big day. We should definitely get donuts with lunch."

"Last week you said that ordering new Post-its was a good enough reason to get donuts," Susannah said. "But okay, we'll think about it."

"Don't worry, we certainly will."

It didn't take Finn long. It took them exactly one day, three hours, and seventeen minutes, unless Susannah's watch was slightly out of time.

"I've got it!"

Susannah half expected them to tack on a "Eureka!" for good measure. "Got what?"

"The perfect night for you. There's a queer ladies' night at the Kilted Coo. You know it, right? Just a couple of towns over that way."

"And that's big enough to host...what? If you say speed dating—"

"Speed dating went out with frosted tips and Hannah Montana, Suze. Honestly, you're like the before part of a rom-com sometimes."

Susannah winced at the accuracy of that one. Maybe she should be staying in with a bowl of popcorn and *Love, Actually*, getting annoyed all over again that the lesbian storyline got cut. "And this place is okay?"

"It's really nice. Not for nothing, but it has some things about it that might be ideas for The Spiky Thistle. If the day should ever come where you want to tart it up a bit."

"Just give me the details, please."

"Already on your calendar. There's a website if you want to see some pictures from previous nights. It's all very classy, no forced rituals and no cheesy games. Just people meeting people and seeing what they might have in common."

"Thank you, Finn. I might be a little embarrassed about all this, but you've been a gem."

"No problem. You off for a ride?"

Susannah looked down at her obvious riding clothes, including the boots, and waved the riding crop in her hand. "That or a costume party where the theme is the Derby, yes."

"You better brush up on your jokes before inflicting them on some unsuspecting woman, Boss. Maybe just lead with how you're rich and have horses. Play to your strengths."

"Thanks for that."

It wasn't often Susannah brought the horses down towards the village. They didn't mind the cobbled streets, not with their solid hooves and sturdy legs, but it meant coming closer to cars and idiotic pedestrians, something she tried to avoid for them whenever possible.

Still, it was important to keep the horses stimulated, and it was as far as she could take Billie Jean from the limited routes she had been following as part of her recuperation. Very successful that had been too since the horse was trotting along like she had never so much as stubbed a toe.

The quickest way back home was down behind the pub and up through the fields, a chance to really work up to a gallop. Susannah idly thought of one of the smaller properties in her portfolio, just down that way. A charming little two-bed with ivy around the door. That one shouldn't even be hers. Jimmy had sworn off buying any more village property after the pub. Then the family who'd been living there had lost their son in some terrible accident, and they wanted to sell up quickly and move somewhere less haunted by memories. Ever the compassionate one, Jimmy had paid them over the odds for it and arranged the movers too, to spare them the cost.

As she bumped along the uneven road, Susannah considered whether she could live up to that example. All the money and decisions on how to spend it were down to her now. Would she help out a neighbour that way, now she could afford to? A straw poll of the villagers would probably not go in her favour, especially lately.

She was almost past the house, with its quaint courtyard and the neighbouring properties that overlooked it, when the front door flew open and Waffles came bounding out. Susannah knew that dog anywhere now, and his owner was becoming just as familiar.

Sure enough, Tess followed the dog out, calling him to heel as soon as she heard the horse's hooves. Then she noticed Susannah was the rider and did that rarest of things in these parts: she actually smiled.

"Coming to check I haven't wrecked the place?" Tess asked.

"Sorry?" Susannah wasn't sure if she should dismount. It seemed a little imperious to be talking down from such a fine, tall horse. Tess wasn't exactly towering; she was barely five-foot-nothing if she was an inch.

"I saw the paperwork. You're my landlady. Suppose it's just as well we made friends, eh?"

"Well, I am glad about that, yes."

"Not as glad as I am. Don't want to be jobless and homeless in one fell swoop. Had enough of that kind of upheaval to last me a lifetime, thank you."

"Ah. That was your ex. Caroline, wasn't it?"

Tess seemed taken aback that Susannah would remember.

"It was only last night, you know. Not such a strain on the memory cells."

"Right, I suppose so."

"Anyway, I seem to remember you taking great offence yesterday to someone thinking you'd be anything less than completely scrupulous. Or did I imagine that shouting match?"

The scrunch of Tess's nose suggested she knew what point was being made. It was really very pretty, the way she did it. Her whole face, actually; it was damned near magnetic in pulling Susannah's attention back to it.

"You're saying you'd expect the same benefit of the doubt be given to you as my landlord, eh?" Tess scuffed a boot against the ground. "That's only fair. I'll stop talking about you like something out of Dickens."

"Never did like Dickens—always reminded me of school," Susannah said. "Of course, I would say that. In Dickens, someone like me is usually the villain. Still, give me Wilkie Collins any day."

"You're quite the nerd, Your Ladyship."

"Enough of that," Susannah warned, giving Tess a mock telling-off by waving the riding crop in her direction. "It's Susannah to you. Maybe one day you'll work your way up to Suze, but we'll see."

"Well, it's important for me to have goals." Tess's smile was progressing to downright cheeky. "Must be getting back to work. Don't want to lose wages in case I can't pay rent. My landlady's a real dragon, you see..."

"Oh, the worst. Breathing fire is the least of your worries."

Tess walked off, laughing, Waffles bounding in large circles around her.

Susannah was more surprised that she was laughing too. When was the last time she felt this light? She started off on the ride home. Maybe she really was ready to get back out there.

Chapter 13

"No, no, no... Would you like me to try it in other languages? *Non. Nein. No.* Oh, well that was a Spanish *no*. You get the point though, yeah?" Tess turned slightly, wary of her position at the top of the ladder, to give Babs the stink-eye.

It wasn't the sturdiest of ladders she had ever worked with, but borrowers couldn't be choosers. Running the pub clearly didn't make for much of a DIY enthusiast. Tess found herself itching for the imminent delivery of all her things, from furniture to fill the empty rooms right down to the toolboxes and personal knick-knacks that would make her new house a home.

"Doc, you should at least consider it," Babs said from where she was sitting on an upturned crate in Tess's new bedroom, reading *The Daily Mirror* and sipping from a huge mug of tea. Considering they'd only hung out twice before, Babs was certainly making herself at home. "That isn't straight, by the way," she added about the curtain rail, looking up for just a moment.

"Yes, it is," Tess replied, but a quick balance of the spirit level confirmed Babs's uncanny eye for these things. "Okay, now it is. Thanks for the curtains. I'll give them back when I work out what I'm doing with this room. But this stops me flashing the neighbours for now."

"Well, that would be quicker than going to some lesbian dating night," Babs said. "But since you're going with curtains and modesty, I'm dragging you out to at least meet people."

Tess came back down the ladder, a little overheated even in her white tank top and cargo shorts. It was warm work, setting up a house. "You know, when I mentioned in the pub the other night that I wanted to meet more people, I meant as friends."

"Right, uh-huh. Can't tell you how many *friends* I've gone looking for at a dating night. Often find myself frustrated for the lack of a good *friendly* chat."

As Tess rolled her eyes and excused herself for the bathroom, her phone rang in the bedroom. "Get that for me, will you? I don't want to change my energy supplier and I haven't been in any accidents."

It only took a couple of minutes to freshen up, but Babs was still chatting away as Tess returned to tackle the next task.

"Yes, of course. Well, it's not really my place to say," Babs was saying. "But we're all very happy to see Tess so happy. Actually, Caroline, it looks like she's just headed out to the car. I'll get her to call you back instead."

"Caroline?" Tess felt her stomach sink towards her knees as Babs ended the call. "You could have just gotten rid of her."

"Oh no, glad I picked up," Babs replied, getting up off the crate. Her brassy hair was pulled up into a formidable top-knot, and she was dressed in comfortable dungarees with a pink T-shirt underneath. "You told me so much about her last time you propped up my bar, and Caroline had a lot to tell me, too. Engaged, is she?"

"Yeah, I was meant to—"

"Not that you'll be bothered about that. What with your new girlfriend and all. Anything you want to tell me?"

"Did you…?"

"I covered for you, don't worry. Although you'll never believe what she thinks your girlfriend's name is."

Tess fumbled for a less embarrassing explanation, but nothing came to mind quickly enough. Did this really have to happen with one of Susannah's great loyalists in the village?

"I mean, I assume from talking to her that Caroline isn't big on things like bothering to get a name right. Asked if you were bringing Susan to her wedding. And I couldn't help thinking that Susan sounds an awful lot like Susannah. Funny that."

Tess took a seat on a crate, squeezing her knees for something to do with her hands.

"Don't you think if I was getting it on with your boss that you'd know about it? Or Margo might have noticed, since I'm still sleeping in her spare room?"

Babs patted Tess on the shoulder, her floral perfume a little overwhelming. "You don't have to make things up. Nice-looking girl like you won't take long to find someone. Susannah could do with the same, but she'll know herself when she's ready."

"I wasn't... Babs, it is really super important that you know this isn't some wishful thinking on my part. The name just came out because I'd been reading about her, and Caroline was talking about me like I'd been permanently taken off the market. It really was just a freak coincidence, so you won't mention it to Susannah, will you?"

"Oh, I'll try my best not to let anything slip. But you're still on the market?" Babs sipped her tea, a twinkle firmly in her eyes.

"I'm still on the market if you promise you won't say anything to your boss about me?"

"Fine, I promise. But you are coming to the big night out at the Kilted Coo, and you're going to get to know some fun new people. All work and no play makes Tess—"

"Tired and gay?" she answered, knowing already it wouldn't be anything like enough to deter Babs.

"You'll have fun. Trust me. And besides, I'm not taking no for an answer."

Tess didn't recall agreeing to giving up a huge chunk of her Friday to get ready for the damn event. How much time could it take to pick out some clothes, a bit of eyeliner, and some hair product? Okay, fine, so she was a little precious about her hair when she wore it down. That part was a little time-consuming.

It also turned out Babs wasn't kidding about making it a group event. When Tess slipped in through the back door of the pub through to the living area, there was already a gaggle of women. Some she'd seen around the village in varying degrees of biker gear or full femme fashion, and a couple were strangers. In the blur of introductions, Tess didn't retain a single name, but the drinks were soon being passed out, and that was invitation enough.

"You brought options?" Babs asked as soon as she swept in from the bar. "Because I don't think work jeans and a T-shirt look like you're making an effort."

"The jeans are nice. Tight," one of the new girls chimed in, but she was already coupled off, leaving Tess to take the compliment at face value and nothing more.

"There's some stuff in my bag," Tess said, sipping at the beer bottle that Babs had handed her. "It's barely half-six; surely we're not heading out already?"

"No, there's time yet." Babs had taken up residence in a grand old armchair. She was certainly glammed up for the occasion, in a dark green dress that put her considerable assets front and centre. Her nails were painted to match. "I'm surprised you didn't bring Margo along for moral support.

"Oh, she wanted to come," Tess replied, unzipping her bag to find a change of clothes. "But in her condition, a whole day on your feet is apparently hard on the swollen-ankle front."

"Having a baby had to start slowing her down eventually," Babs said. "Go on, bathroom's through there if you want to do your quick change. It won't be so scary out there, Doc. We're all just going out to let our hair down."

By the time she was dressed, hogging the guest bathroom for as long as she thought she could get away with, Tess quite liked the look of herself. Letting her hair down—literally—offset the roundness of her face more. At least the smoky eyes with a bit of lip gloss looked like she'd done it on purpose. Margo had still had some influence, since this outfit of black ripped jeans and a sleeveless top had been her pick.

Tess re-entered the living room to a round of applause and wolf whistles that didn't even sound sarcastic. It was a bit of an ego boost, even as she waved away the attention. "Ready?" she asked the assembled throng that, at a glance, spanned most of the queer lady spectrum.

There was a collective raising of glasses and bottles in answer.

"Okay, one more drink, then we start calling for cabs, yeah?" Tess suggested.

The collective cheer said she was on the right track.

The pub was very nice, in fairness, and Tess could see why Joan had recommended it. Far more spacious than the Thistle, it also seemed to have been decorated at some point since the end of the Second World War. They were far from the first to arrive, and Tess was impressed that a relatively small Borders town could draw such a diverse crowd on a weekend.

As she waited at the bar, she realised that tonight was something of an event. People had come from miles around. Tess imagined it was an alternative to plotting overnight plans in the big cities of Edinburgh and Glasgow.

"First time?" the barmaid asked. Her hair was bubblegum pink, shaved on one side. The nametag on her shirt, *Lizzie*, was affixed to just about the only unripped or pinned bit of fabric.

Tess didn't need to look past the hotpants and fishnets to be sure there would be a beat-up pair of Doc Martens. She knew punk when she saw it. "That obvious?" Tess replied. "Mine's a pint of bitter, and I was going to order for my friends, but they've already wandered off."

"Don't worry. You'll get the hang of it quickly enough. Just watch out for the barflies. They get here early, and they're just looking for someone to pick up the tab. The baby dykes tend to colonise the pool table, so proceed with caution if you want a game."

Tess shook her head. "And if I give you my star sign, think you could pick out my soulmate while you're at it?"

"If I could do that at a glance, do you think I'd be back here cleaning glasses? Now, you always get a few straight-girl tourists, which is ridiculous." Lizzie pointed to the gaggle at the door who were laughing into their cocktails. "They don't tend to be much trouble, and it gives them a night out without being chased by men. You just here to scout the scene, or are you on the pull for real?"

"You...don't mess around with the questions, do you?" Tess accepted her drink and took a grateful sip. "I'm not sure yet. My new friend basically dragged me by the hair, so we'll see."

"Well, enjoy. Anyone gives you trouble, you just flag me down. Most of them know better than to piss off Lizzie."

Tess nodded and slipped away to lose herself in the gathering crowd. She wasn't exactly scouring for potential dates, but a few women caught her eye as she passed. She might not have had that skinny, androgynous look that always seemed to be in demand, but there were some appreciative glances at Tess that suggested a curve or two was very much in favour around here.

And there was no shortage of sassy barmaids in the Borders, either. Tess saw Babs and Lizzie comparing notes over the bar, cracking each other up laughing in the process. All over the large venue, people were already pairing off or settling into familiar groups. The music was almost drowned out by the noise of everyone talking, probably a mercy given that it was cheesy Europop, from the little Tess could hear.

She took a longer drink, setting up camp by one of the pillars that ran down the centre of the room. It was a perfect vantage point, one from which she could see almost everything without pulling too much attention to herself. She checked her phone as one song blended into another, and despite a lot of glances at the fresh meat, nobody seemed interesting in approaching her. Tess had a feeling she'd have to do the legwork herself.

Great. That was going to take another drink.

It wasn't that hard in the end. Babs came over to rescue Tess from her lonely posturing and introduced some of the other regulars. She left Tess with a wink as she went back to chatting up an older woman at the bar, and it was actually fun to hear how people had come from all sorts of backgrounds, different jobs, and different places.

Okay, so maybe nobody gave Tess that little thrill of first attraction, but meeting all these new people made her realise how much space there was in her life for them.

Had she been lonely all this time without being aware of it?

On that bleak discovery, she realised that the noise and the heat of all these bodies was getting to her. Having shrugged off her leather jacket earlier, she snagged it and headed for the back door. For a moment, she could have sworn she saw Finn, but given that they were all loved-up with Dave, it was less than likely.

Stepping out into the car park, Tess couldn't help wishing she still smoked. It was always useful as a way to guarantee a few minutes away from stressful situations. Unless, of course, she got cornered by some other stranger seeking a light, which often happened just as she was starting to feel more peaceful.

At the tap on her shoulder, she turned, saying, "Sorry, I don't..." The person seeking her attention was the last one she expected.

"Don't worry. I'm not asking to bum a smoke. Didn't expect to see you here, of all people." Susannah looked a little cold in her sleeveless blue dress, the thin belt around her waist just a sliver of gold.

For a chivalrous moment, Tess wondered if she should offer her jacket. "Really? Why wouldn't I be?"

"Just don't get the Friday night meat market vibe from you. That was a compliment, I suppose?"

"Careful, I might start thinking you really don't hate me after all."

Susannah rubbed her bare arms. "I thought we'd been over that. Very insecure of you to go fishing again, Doctor."

"Oh, here." Chivalry won out in the end. Tess shrugged her jacket off and slipped it over Susannah's shoulders before she could argue. "I can handle a bit of a nip in the air. I was born to it, wasn't I?"

"It's not like Cheshire is known for being a tropical paradise," Susannah argued. "This is a nice jacket. I might not give it back."

"Not in a hurry to head back in, then?" Tess didn't know quite what she was asking, but there was a charge in the air all of a sudden, one that made the fine hairs on her forearms stand up.

"Do you know, I think I'm fine where I am." Susannah leaned against the wall and gave Tess a small, lovely smile.

Chapter 14

She should not have been out here.

Finn's instructions were perfectly simple: go in, get a drink, and just take a look around. Susannah hadn't managed to follow even those simple steps.

Now she was leaning against the wall in a borrowed jacket that smelled of some light, woody perfume mingled with the unmistakable scent of good leather, and all these facts were conspiring to make her smile. A real cheesy, uncontrollable, cheek-muscle-stretching grin. For a while there, she'd thought her face had forgotten how.

"You do seem fine. Where you are," Tess finally replied.

Was she… Oh, she was blushing all right. That fair complexion all redheads seemed to have really showed up the embarrassment too.

"If you don't want to head in, maybe we could go for a walk?" Tess continued. "I get the feeling this might be a popular spot for, um…"

Susannah giggled. Actually out-loud giggled. She hadn't touched a drop of alcohol, and yet she was strangely light-headed. "Oh yes, quite. Wouldn't want to cramp anyone's style. Looks like that path leads down to the river?"

"It's a burn, actually." It was pleasant how Tess's Scottish burr wrapped around the word. "Or a brook, I suppose, where you're from."

"Didn't realise vets took a linguistics course." Susannah pushed away from the wall, leading the way to the burn. "You do keep surprising me."

Tess fell in step without seeming to try.

It had been too long since Susannah did something as simple as go for a walk with another person; too often she rambled around the estate on her own.

"How do you do that?" Tess asked. "You're just talking about something, like the fact that I surprise you, but it always sounds like an accusation. I feel like I've been caught with my hand in the biscuit tin when I talk to you. Most of the time."

"Forgive me," Susannah said, and It was suddenly very urgent that Tess did. "I'm out of practice."

"At what?"

"You name it: talking to people normally, making a friend, being around other people. I could put it all down to grief, or a tough year in general, but the truth is I've always been just awful at it. Honestly, I'm much better with horses than people."

"I think there's some hope for you yet." Tess stared out over the narrow body of water. Their pace slowed to a stroll. "When we're not sniping at each other, talking to you is actually quite pleasant. Not that I'd run around admitting that, of course. I suppose you're used to everyone bowing and scraping as well. Can't make it easy to go out and get hammered with people, and that's how I used to meet new folk. Never quite worked out how to do that after uni, though."

"You've worked your charms on Babs," Susannah replied, choosing her words carefully. "It's not just anyone she'll bring on a wild night out. I'm surprised she hasn't gone after you herself."

"I don't think I'm her type." Tess opened her mouth as if to follow the thought but seemed to change her mind.

"You never know what people do and don't like. I know I'm an acquired taste, for instance. Even my sister-in-law seems to hate me these days, but I swear we used to get on before. I told myself grief does strange things to people. It's only getting stranger."

They came to a bench overlooking the widest part of the burn. Susannah didn't feel like sitting; her legs had miles in them yet. Instead she leaned against the back of it. A moment later, Tess followed her cue to do the same. The water trickled on behind them, like a real-life mediation scene.

"Is that why you're letting her get away with it?" Tess asked, her voice barely audible above the sounds of the water, the trees rustling, and the distant rumble and honks of the main road somewhere ahead of them. "Or hoping she'll just stop it, anyway? I figured it was out of respect for your husband."

"Not my style," Susannah said, and even if they never talked again, she wanted Tess to understand that much. "And in the interests of this new friendship we have, I think there's a rumour or two worth addressing. Jimmy and I, we were a partnership, a good one. But our relationship wasn't a romantic one. I get the feeling you've picked up on that."

Tess nodded. "I really don't mean to pry. It's just you're a popular topic of conversation around Hayleith. I take a lot of it with a pinch of salt. You should do the same, if they ever talk about me."

"I will. I should have done more to become part of village life, I see that now. Nobody likes the snooty noblewoman up there in her ivory tower. Maybe it's not too late, once I make some big changes around the estate. Meanwhile, attacking Robin buys me nothing and risks quite a lot. If I keep to the high road, in public at least, then I have an advantage over her."

"So you're saying you don't need someone to go round and take a hockey stick to her car?"

"Are you volunteering?"

"Where would I get one?" Tess asked. "You might be all jolly hockey sticks, but I went to the kind of schools where sporting equipment was banned in case it was used for weapons. That, and they couldn't afford much of it in the first place."

Susannah gave a wry smile. Although her father had run out of money at regular intervals, she had always made it back to school eventually. The odd relative had paid for nice holidays too, so there had always been something to look forward to. She knew better than to patronise Tess by pretending she could relate.

"Well, I'll just thank you for the offer. And if I root around in my wardrobes, I might be able to find you a hockey stick, should the occasion arise. I might even have my old uniform in there too."

Tess turned fully around at that, her grin far more than friendly. "Tell me you're not talking about those tiny skirts and vest tops. Because that's really not fair."

"Fair?" Susannah could play dumb when it suited her. "Didn't realise you were such a sports fan, Tess."

That just made her laugh. It felt pretty damn nice, actually, having the power to do that. It was certainly a lovely laugh.

"Still, no vigilante justice for now," Susannah continued. "I'll get my way—because most of the time I do—and then afterwards I'll see if I can mend some bridges. Believe it or not, I don't actually like having people out to get me."

"I can see that would be exhausting."

"It is." Susannah could get used to this feeling of being understood for a change. "It's good you're resourceful. If you really want to go fighting my battles, I'm sure you could lay your hands on something."

Whoops. That wasn't intended to sound quite so flirty, but it was certainly getting a blush to rise on Tess's cheeks again.

This close, side-by-side, Susannah could see the light sprinkling of freckles that dusted Tess's nose and cheekbones. She had that rarest of things: a perfect nose. Not too long or too rounded. No bumps or deviations. It's what a surgeon would surely pick out as the default model, if such a thing existed.

"I suppose I am good with my hands," Tess replied, although the long pause made it seem more of a defence than a witty comeback. "Isn't being here with me reducing your chances of meeting someone? I assume someone dragged you to the dating pool, like Babs did with me?"

"There's no rush." Susannah rubbed her hands on the sides of her thighs. "This is just—what would you call it—an opening salvo. First step on a long path, that sort of thing."

"So, just to be absolutely clear, with you coming to a night like this and all…and not wanting to go on rumours alone, are you actually interested in dating women? Only with you being married to a man for years…"

Well, well, well. Isn't the good doctor getting brave? That was downright direct for her. "Like I said before, my marriage was more of an arrangement between two people who didn't feel able to pursue…other relationships. My family was whatever the opposite of supportive is when I first got caught showing an interest in girls. Jimmy offered me a safe route away from that, and a nice comfortable life to go with it. We were happy, though."

For once, telling the truth about her situation didn't feel disloyal. It felt like finally being honest after too many years of shoving it down or talking around it. "And while I'm talking openly with you about it, this hasn't been public knowledge until recently. Or, at least, I haven't confirmed it to anyone."

"I was just asking." Tess held her hands up.

They kept doing this, the thrust and parry of argument leading to surrender. For a moment, Susannah's shoulders slumped. She was so tired. Why was she out tonight, trying to start all over again?

"You're quite a catch, you know," Tess continued. "I'm surprised you made it through the bar without picking up a date."

"That was some impressive flattery." Susannah said it with a smile. It took a lot of work to look like this, especially into her forties. She was used to compliments, maybe even expected them in a lot of contexts, but Tess had a way of seeming like she really meant it. "Not that you have to stop."

"Susannah, I—"

It was just a kiss. Susannah decided to do it in the same split second as actually pressing her lips to Tess's. There was no plan, no premeditation at all beyond avoiding another tricky conversation. It could have been ridiculous, a mistimed gesture that had Tess backing away or laughing in her face. Instead, Susannah found herself being kissed back in that spine-tingling way when two instinctive kissers find themselves suddenly aligned.

There was a momentary clash of noses, a mutual adjustment of angles to line their mouths up right, but the soft, insistent pressure of each overlapping kiss was as constant as it was delicious.

"Wow." Tess had her eyes closed when she finally leaned away. It took her a moment to open them. "Of all the things I expected tonight…"

"Maybe it was my turn to be surprising. You're pretty good at that too. If you're keeping any kind of score."

"I really want to do that again." Tess started to lean in.

Susannah was all for it, but just as she moved to repeat that very pleasant experience, she caught sight of someone on the path. It was no reason to stop; she knew that even as she froze.

The person—a man, and no one she recognised—was coming from the opposite direction to the pub. Common sense said carry on, but Tess had already pulled back, her expression thoroughly wounded and rejected.

"I, uh…" Susannah began.

"No, I get it," Tess said with a sigh that seemed to come all the way from the lightly scuffed biker boots she was wearing. "Impulse decisions sometimes wear off. You can have that one as a free bad idea."

Susannah could see the moment slipping away and knew on some level that she could claw back the beautiful moment if only she tried. "No, no, I didn't change my mind. I'm just...catching my breath?"

"Wow, as excuses go that is...wow. Listen, I get it. Passing impulses happen to the best of us. Then you remembered people can actually see us out here and thought your fancy reputation might take a hit from snogging the lowly local vet. A *female* lowly vet at that."

"Tess—"

"Honestly, it's fine. I'm not offended." For someone not offended, Tess could have appeared next to its definition in the dictionary. "Probably just the pressure of the whole dating night. You just forgot yourself for a moment, and I was in the right place at what turned out to be the wrong time."

"Tess, no—" Susannah reached for Tess's arm, but she was already in motion, moving away from their shared bench. "It's really nothing personal," she said, but it sounded half-hearted even to her own ears. "And I'm done hiding who I am now—that's what coming somewhere like this was about in the first place—so it wasn't a reaction to being *caught*. And it's certainly nothing to do with you being a vet; I don't know where you got that idea. I just...paused. That's hardly a crime. Listen, maybe we could start this over. Why don't I buy you a drink and then we can see—"

"Let's not mess things up more than we almost did, yeah?" Tess held out her hand. "Wouldn't mind my jacket back, actually. We can put it all down to the persuasive effects of a really cool jacket."

"Oh, take the jacket!" Susannah's temper spiked as she yanked it from her shoulders. Cool as the air around her was, she refused to shiver while Tess could see it. "But I really think you're being too harsh, making this all about class. Or money, or whatever you're implying. If I was such a stuck-up cow, I never would have had any such impulse in the first place. So you see—"

"Well, thank you for explaining the vagaries of the British class system to me. This has just served as a timely reminder why I don't go in for all that bowing and scraping. I'd say your moment of reconsidering has probably saved us both a lot of time and embarrassment. This was clearly a terrible idea." She waved a hand between them. Then Tess was on the move, striding back along the path towards the Kilted Coo.

The pub was full of eligible women, all of whom would probably have handled this situation much better than that. Yet for all Susannah's shame and annoyance, she couldn't help running her fingertip over her bottom lip. Still tingling. Still waiting for a repeat performance of that kiss. It was going to have to wait a long time, judging by that exit.

Susannah pulled out her phone to text Finn. Even with a considerable gap in her dating record, women hadn't become any less maddening. Of all the unnecessary things to take umbrage over, *really*.

Tess was obviously fixated on their different social standings or she wouldn't have brought it up in the first place. It had been the farthest thing from Susannah's mind. Of course the damned woman hadn't been concerned about their respective tax brackets when she'd been kissing her back so enthusiastically. Pride. Bloody pride.

It stung even more that Tess had zeroed right in on Susannah's own history of shame around her sexuality, and that she'd managed to do it on a night when Susannah thought she might finally have moved past all that residual self-loathing and hiding. Still, it just showed that this had all been a grand mistake and that it was time to get back to the safety of Midsummer.

Chapter 15

Tess was tempted to ignore the email from Finn, but anything at her work address was visible to any of the other partners.

Besides, a day of looking at horses in need of retirement homes sounded like it could be good for the soul. Even if she was having to do it in the company of the woman who kissed her a couple of weeks ago, and then rejected her in the space of five minutes.

It would have been very cool, not to mention incredibly mature, if Tess could say she hadn't given that debacle a moment's thought since. Unfortunately, it had been the one thing she couldn't stop thinking about. Susannah might present that stuck-up image to the world, but she kissed more beautifully than she had any right to.

Tess stabbed at the phone screen with her thumbs as she replied.

Ok. Just let me know what time to pick up S and we'll go from there.

Lady Kiss-and-Change-Her-Mind would assume they were going in her car, but Tess was still feeling defensive about hers. It was perfectly capable of doing the job, and if she had to be out for hours with someone who kissed her and then thought better of it, then she was at least going to have home-court advantage. And control over the music.

Turning back to her coffee, Tess shoved her phone back in her pocket and contemplated the carrot cake Joan was putting in the glass display case with the same care and attention as a woman who'd been charged with cleaning the Crown Jewels.

"If you're going to ask for a slice, do it before I close this case again," Joan said when she caught Tess staring. "But what you really want is one of these strawberry tarts." She nodded to the small tray containing six little mountains of juicy strawberries, shining under their sticky-sweet red syrup.

Tess reddened. They looked glorious, and her tummy gurgled in agreement.

"You're blushing at a cake?" Joan asked as Tess came over to the counter.

"No, it's just...it's silly." Tess shook her head. "'Strawberry tart' was just a stupid thing people used to call me in school. No one as witty as teenagers, eh?"

"And were you?" Joan asked, a hint of challenge to the question. "A tart?"

"I think it was supposed to be ironic. Wasn't exactly dating up a storm back then. Don't think I knew what a lesbian was, never mind that I was one."

Joan made a little scoffing noise, but she slid a tart onto a plate for Tess. "This one's on me."

"What for? I mean, thank you. But why?" Tess never had learned *not* to look a gift horse in the mouth.

"I heard what you did for Mrs Thompson last week with her cat. Plenty of people would have made her come to the surgery, but she wasn't fit for that. It was kinder, letting the poor puss go at home."

Tess nodded. Being able to reach most patients within a few minutes made simple acts of compassion much easier to offer, and the appointments at this practice weren't crammed back-to-back like they had been in her old surgery. It didn't hurt that home visits made the worst part of her job a little easier.

"It's the least I could do. Do you look in on her? I'm worried she'll be lonely."

"I do. We look after each other here; you're getting to see that." She paused. "I'll be honest, Dr Robinson. I wasn't sure about you when you first rocked up to Hayleith. But apart from your poor taste in drinking establishments, you're settling in nicely."

Tess wanted to protest that she wasn't going to another town entirely when the pub was right next to her house, but she knew enough to bite her tongue. "It's nice to be so welcomed. I can really see myself settling here, especially now that my house has furniture and I actually have all my clothes again."

"You'd be even more settled if you met a nice young lady. No luck at the Kilted Coo?"

There was a knowing glint in Jean's eye. For someone who hadn't even been there, she seemed quite aware that something had gone on.

"No, it was a bit much for me in the end. All that showing off and parading around looking for dates? I ended up going for a walk. I'll just take this over—"

"Go anywhere nice on your walk? There are some *lovely* trails around there." Joan prepared another coffee without Tess having to ask. "You shouldn't wander off on your own, mind."

"Oh, I was perfectly safe. And I didn't say I went alone," Tess replied, throwing in a little wink for good measure. "I wouldn't be picking out a hat for the wedding, though, if you catch my drift."

She expected a witty remark in response, but instead Joan looked straight over her shoulder and said, "Hello there, Lady Karlson. Usual is it?"

Let her be kidding. Let it be an elaborate set-up to confirm a lucky guess. Tess risked turning around, hoping she would see nothing but a half-empty café behind her. She knew as she did that her hope was unfounded, because she could smell that rich, distinctive perfume and expensive shampoo that she got to experience up close by that bench.

Susannah's expression was inscrutable. She had her wallet in one hand and with the other she was patting Waffles' head, because of course the big fluffy traitor had come to get attention but didn't think to alert his devoted owner to anyone else's presence.

"Just a double espresso today, Joan. To go."

"I'll get out of the way," Tess said. "Waffles, stop bothering people. Sorry, he really doesn't give you much choice once he knows you like him."

"I don't mind," Susannah replied.

Waffles gave Tess a reproachful look with his big brown eyes, staying put at Susannah's side.

Joan turned her attention to Susannah, nodding to Tess as she did. "Dr Robinson here was just telling me about the lovely time she had at the big LGBT night out the other week. Didn't you mention something about that?"

"I might have mentioned that Finn was trying to drag me there, yes," Susannah replied.

"You two might well have bumped into each other, then," Joan persisted, as she worked the machine to produce the requested coffee. "Or crossed paths, if you will."

"I really do have to be getting on." Susannah set some cash on top of the counter and almost snatched the paper cup from Joan's hand as soon as she offered it.

"We're going out to see those horses tomorrow, yeah?" Tess should have let Susannah escape as quickly as possible, but some annoying little impulse asked the question to make her stick around.

"If that's what the calendar says, then yes. I understand if you're too busy."

"Not at all. Finn's letting me know what time to collect you."

"But—"

"Thanks for the strawberry tart, Joan." Tess picked up the plate and her coffee, relieved when Waffles followed her back to the table. His first loyalty would always be to snacks he thought he could steal.

For a moment, it looked as though Susannah would swing by Tess's table to argue about who would get to drive, but instead she sauntered out on those long legs, forcing Tess to keep her eyes front and not appreciate the sight of Susannah Karlson walking away.

Tess was ten minutes early, so she killed the engine and took a proper look at the Midsummer mansion from the front. She must have been right in her previous assessment of at least ten bedrooms. The two wings of the house were as grand as each other, and Tess found herself speculating which of those huge windows marked Susannah's bedroom.

Years ago, when it had first opened to summer tours, Caroline had dragged Tess around Buckingham Palace with a bunch of tourists. While they'd all seemed fascinated by antique tea sets and heavy silk drapes, Tess had spent most of the time counting down the minutes until they'd be free to leave. She'd never been dazzled by opulence.

Did Susannah have one of those ridiculous four-poster beds? Not that Tess would get to see it anytime soon, not when they couldn't make it to a second kiss. What did someone even put in all those other rooms? Was there a gym? Susannah obviously worked out and…huh. That kiss had really done a number on Tess's attention span when it came to the lady of the manor.

She was just debating if there was time to nip down to the stables and say a quick hello to the horses, who hadn't needed much attention from her since Billie Jean's leg recovered, when Susannah came marching out the front door.

The look today was every bit the country gentlewoman: Creamy jodhpurs, pulled taut across Susannah's shapely thighs, disappeared into those familiar riding boots. On top, the lightly quilted navy Barbour jacket was buttoned and belted, but it offered a glimpse of grey cashmere under it. No riding helmet, since they were just going to look at horses, but Susannah had her hair back in a low bun.

She stopped just short of the car and gave it a once-over, shaking her head slowly before opening the passenger door and easing her way in. "You're on time. Good," was her idea of a greeting. "Sure this thing can handle the rougher roads? This farm really is in the back of the beyond. We'll be almost in England."

"Oh no, not England," Tess deadpanned. She started the car, and of course it decided not to take first time. Muttering curses under her breath, she tried again. This time the engine roared into life. With just a sideways glance at Susannah's doubtful expression, Tess jabbed at the sound system and let the playlist she'd been listening to remove any need for conversation.

They were all the way down the long driveway and onto the main road before Susannah reached out and turned the volume back down.

"Do you mind?" Tess could adjust it back up from the steering wheel, but she was too curious about whether Susannah wanted to talk. Maybe she was just being territorial and petty. It certainly wouldn't be the first time.

"Melissa Etheridge? Really? Were they all out of new CDs at the cliché factory?"

They passed the pub and both raised a hand to wave to Babs as she stood outside arguing with a delivery driver.

"First of all, it's a playlist, so she's not the only one on there. Secondly, Melissa is a legend, and I won't stand for besmirching her name in this car."

"Besmirching?"

"You know what I mean. I'm sure you'd rather we listened to something classical on a BBC station, but some of us like a song you can sing along to." Tess let her speed pick up as they got out of the populated part of town. It was all long and winding roads from here. She almost always checked her routes before driving anywhere, scrolling through her map app like she'd be tested on it. If only she'd been so diligent on the day she arrived in Hayleith.

"You don't know the first thing about my music tastes," Susannah replied, reverting back to that frosty voice she usually reserved for her meddling sister-in-law. "For all you know, I could be the karaoke queen of the Scottish Borders."

"I hate karaoke."

"That's like saying you hate fun," Susannah said, and it was genuinely impossible to tell whether she was serious or not.

Tess lapsed into the silence, letting Melissa give way to Pat Benatar, which Susannah actually hummed along to.

Only the SatNav spoke for the next few miles, before curiosity got the better of Tess. "This one of your standards at karaoke, then?" she asked.

Susannah exhaled loudly in dismissal. Right, so she was just playing games, then. "I'm more of a Cher person, actually. Needs to be something you can really belt out."

Tess gave her a quick look, but Susannah was focused on the road ahead, apparently deadly serious. "Well, forgive me if I say I'll believe that when I see it."

"Fine. I'll have Babs arrange one of her infamous karaoke nights. Of course, you'll have to sing too, otherwise there's no deal."

"Sure," Tess felt confident in her assessment now. "I'll be right up there. Right after you. Maybe I'll go country. Dolly Parton?"

"Not sure you have the chest for that," Susannah said, although it was more like she was muttering it to herself.

Tess wriggled a little beneath her seatbelt. It wasn't like she wanted to be super busty, but she was hardly flat-chested. Most importantly, Susannah was the one bringing up physical attributes, which suggested she'd been thinking about them. Point one to Tess. It was just a shame she had no idea what they were playing, how the points were really awarded, or what a win would look like.

"If you want to stop for coffee or something at any point, I don't mind," Susannah piped up a bit later, turning the music down. "It's the least I can provide, if you're driving."

"It's okay, I'm billing you for the time, remember?"

"Right. Isn't it nice we're back on familiar ground, Doctor?" Susannah folded her arms over her chest, looking out the side window.

If Tess didn't know better, she might have thought Susannah's feelings were hurt this time. They did keep stumbling into each other that way, finding every sharp edge that hadn't been sanded away yet, falling over every tripwire when it came to volatile topics. "Just keeping the business side ticking over," Tess offered. "Doesn't mean it isn't…nice to be going out with you today."

That got her a pointed look, but Tess concentrated on the light traffic in front of them.

"You made it sound like a chore earlier," Susannah said.

"Going to see some new horses isn't a chore. And neither is being around you. Just because of that little mistake the other week…well, doesn't mean we can't still be friends. We obviously need a bit of practice at it."

"Was it?" Susannah asked after a moment, staring resolutely at the road ahead as though she were the one driving. "A mistake for you? Only you seemed fine with the idea until you got the wrong end of the stick."

Tess gripped the steering wheel harder. Great. Nothing made humiliation more fun than reliving it. "I gave you a pass at the time, Your Ladyship. You did something. You regretted it. Sure, you got those regrets a little quicker than most, but I understand."

"I'm beginning to see you don't understand at all," Susannah replied, snippy again.

Unfortunately snippy and bossy both looked extremely good on her. Time for Tess to stare dead ahead, Susannah's gaze burning into her cheek.

"If you had listened to my explanation, you'd have heard that it was nothing to do with regret," Susannah said. "In fact, I don't regret it even now, despite you being utterly impossible."

"It's coming up on the right," Tess said, beating the SatNav to it by a few seconds. "And what do you mean you don't regret it? Nobody ducks out of a second kiss like that with no reason."

"I *did* have a reason. I was pausing, and it wasn't about you. It was just...reacting to you. To that kiss. And it was very much worth taking a moment to reflect on. Until you jumped to the wrong conclusion, anyway."

Tess told herself it was the bassline of the song hammering in her ears, but it was barely audible. The kiss wasn't a regret. The kiss really had been worth taking a moment to appreciate. Did that mean Tess and her temper had skipped out much too soon? Did she really dare hope that the hot, powerful lady of the manor might still be open to yet further kissing? That was definitely something to find out. Preferably not while operating a moving vehicle.

"Well, it was the only conclusion available to me in the moment." Tess had to hope that sounded like enough of an apology without actually being one.

Susannah opened her mouth as if she was going to argue, but she cleared her throat and nodded instead. "This is it," she said. "We're here."

Chapter 16

As journeys went, it hadn't been as excruciating as it might have been. Still, Susannah practically jumped out of the car the moment it came to a stop. The ground was muddy even right outside the farmhouse, and she suspected the reason these horses were available would be purely financial.

Tess took the lead without having to be asked—that easy way she had of connecting with people, leaving Susannah at a disadvantage. While it probably didn't help with her standoffish reputation, it at least gave her a chance to watch Tess, to see her lay on the easy charm and show off her knowledge as they walked out to the paddock. Two grand black horses were wandering around, content in each other's company.

"We're moving up to town, where our son has his house. Done well for himself," the farmer was explaining, beaming with pride, even though he looked exhausted, in his overalls and flat cap. His beard was patchy and his fingers were stained with nicotine. "My wife always said as soon as the farm got too much work, she wanted a touch of the good life. I owe her that much by now."

"And you don't have any other livestock?" Tess ducked through the paddock fence to approach the horses.

"No, all sold on now. Or slaughtered. Sorry," he added, nodding to Susannah, clearly deciding she had delicate sensibilities. "Just how it is on a working farm."

"I'm well aware, thank you." Susannah cringed at how uptight she sounded and followed Tess through the wooden bars, swinging her leg through without much thought.

Having made her initial assessment, Tess looked up. "They're both in good shape." She looked all business in her rainproof coat and black jeans, her wellies relatively clean of mud considering the trek across the field. "I forgot to ask their names."

"I'll probably rename them if they'll listen," Susannah said, as the taller of the black horses came over to give her an appraising sniff. She held her palm out flat, a hunk of carrot already pulled from her pocket in anticipation. "I don't want another stable full of tennis players, all the same."

"Hmm, this fella has a bit of a bumpy hip," Tess said, running her hand over it. "Minor stuff, though, and it's not affecting his gait. They still have some resale value, so you should make him a fair offer."

"Oh, there's plenty of life in them yet. What do you say, boys? Would you like to come and roam around at Midsummer? We'll take very good care of you. Yes, we will."

"You really love your horses, don't you?"

Susannah gave Tess a withering look. Love wasn't about how many stupid voices you used to talk to an animal. It was giving them care and shelter and looking after them well, giving them a life without worry, even if they'd had a tough start. The rest was just for fun. "Why didn't you bring Waffles? He's good around horses, isn't he?"

"He's good around everyone, if they have food or attention to give. I just never know if the other animals will take to him, so for the most part he hangs around the surgery when I'm in the field."

"Doesn't he miss you?"

"He does, but I make up for it with fussing and treats. Also he's a bit of an unofficial therapy dog. He likes to supervise the inpatients and helps them calm down a bit when their owners first have to leave them. Margo seems to think it's helping, anyway."

Susannah clutched her chest, almost mocking, but she was genuinely moved. "Your dog is a credit to you. Probably more than you deserve, actually." Her lips curled in amusement. "Shall we go and tell this man we'll solve his last problem?"

"Selling the farm is the last problem. Not much property shifting around here at the moment," Tess said, falling in step as they headed back to the fence. "He'll have to hope someone is ready to start out on their own. Maybe workers from a nearby estate."

Susannah didn't know anyone in that position, but she suspected Dave might. She'd have to get Finn on the case as soon as they got back. With that in mind, she offered two hundred over what she'd already agreed, getting an impressed little murmur from Tess in the process. Better this than healthy enough horses being sent to the knacker's yard.

Arrangements were made for collection, and Susannah had a spring in her step as they walked back to the car. "Should I take these off?" She gestured to her boots as Tess sat in the driver's seat, side on, changing her wellies back to more practical running shoes.

"No, the mats will catch it," Tess said, throwing her own boots in the back and gesturing to the black rubber on the floor. "Doubt anyone in this part of the world can keep their car interior all that clean. Don't worry about it. Besides, those are some great boots."

"They are, aren't they?" Susannah's mood improved by the second. Compliments certainly didn't hurt. "Oh, I'm so glad we did this."

"You'll have two more stalls filled by Tuesday," Tess replied. "That's a good start."

"It is. In fact, it's the real start—of everything. I've spent all this time talking and plotting, but this is a milestone, the first real change on the estate that I've done all by myself."

"Take that, wicked sister-in-law!" Tess added a little victory whoop as she started the car.

It cooperated immediately this time, but Susannah didn't miss Tess's little sigh of relief. In all honesty, it was a perfectly fine car—a little showy and overdone with accessories maybe—but it had been fun to tease Tess about it all the same. A lot of things to do with Tess kept turning out to be fun, well, apart from kisses that turned into misunderstandings. Susannah didn't know whether they'd actually resolved that misunderstanding fully, but it was very bloody nice to see Tess's smile once more. Maybe Susannah not saying too much for once was the way to go. Action had always been much more her forte, anyway.

"Now, I think I saw a pub not far from here on the way in," Susannah said. "I know you can't have anything while you're driving, but would you indulge me? Your orange juice is absolutely on me."

"Of course." Tess steered with quiet confidence as they zoomed along the narrow road. "You mean the one set back from the road, with all the trees?"

"It looked decent. And I'm starting to think I should be getting some inspiration for finally overhauling the Thistle." *Wow. Where did that idea come from?* Yet as soon as she said it, Susannah realised the notion had been brewing for a little while. Change forced on her had been difficult and upsetting, but *choosing* to change things felt a lot like power. Actually, it felt a lot like freedom.

They parked out front and entered through a side door, instantly charmed by the rustic interior of the country pub. Susannah made good on her promise, getting the drinks straight away. She was pleased to see Tess choose a table with low sofas in the far end of the pub. There weren't many people in the bar so early in the afternoon, and they had almost complete privacy. A huge fireplace dominated the space, and on a colder day, it would undoubtedly have a roaring fire.

"You should have ordered champagne," Tess sipped her orange juice without complaint. "Celebration and all that."

"I would have, but it doesn't quite seem the sort of place to do it by the glass. Drinking a bottle alone would be..."

"Tragic?"

"You said it. Maybe you could join me to split a bottle some time when you don't have to be behind the wheel." Oh. There was that flirting again. Susannah had sprung into action before even she'd even noticed.

"What are we doing?" Tess asked, instantly on guard.

"I honestly don't know. I'm a little giddy, and here we are in a quiet little nook, miles from home, just this little table between us... I know I was the one to hit pause before—"

"Still, it didn't feel like a pause. It felt like you slammed the stop button, then standby, and unplugged the whole thing for good measure."

"So you're saying that you *were* up for more?" Susannah tried for some levity. "I know I totally tensed up and ruined the moment. Perhaps I could have explained better, but you were quite ready to damn me for it all the same."

"Then fine. It's possible I ever so slightly overreacted." Tess replied, setting her glass down and rubbing her hands on her thighs as though they were cold. Her ponytail swung behind her head as she wriggled in her seat a little. "And I'm the first to admit I do have some sore spots around powerful women, specifically ones with power over me. The whole point of me leaving London and starting over was to get away from a compromised situation. I swore I wouldn't get entangled in anything that affected my job or my living arrangements. You'd have even more control over those than Caroline did. In a way."

"But the difference is I don't want that power. I don't have any bad intentions for using it that way. And you deserve better than that."

"It's just..." Tess seemed genuinely conflicted for a moment.

Susannah's breath hitched when Tess rose from the comfortable chair opposite and came to sit on the same high-backed couch as Susannah.

"It's just..."

"Just what?" Susannah almost whispered, not wanting to shatter the fragile moment. Her wine glass rested in her left hand, all but forgotten. A glance around the room confirmed they were still alone, not a single other soul in sight.

"I guess all of that is really important to me. So important. But then you kissed me, and I thought maybe it wasn't that important at all."

"I'm not your boss," Susannah reminded her. "And your house—there's a contract and an agency and all these layers. And I just want to state right now, that even if I hesitate for a second after I kiss you, I still intend to do it again, if that clears up any confusion?"

"I guess?" Tess slid a few inches closer across the soft seat.

This close, Susannah could see how shallow her breathing was, that her pupils were just that little bit bigger, and darker. The freckles were less hidden—no make-up for a day out in the fields. It was so easy for Susannah to reach across and brush Tess's fringe aside where it had fallen over one eye.

"Maybe we just needed this little bit of privacy," Susannah said, licking her lips quickly. She tasted the hint of oak and peach from her wine. "To work out what matters, and what doesn't. Maybe you can't get past who I am. Maybe I won't get past the way you call me out at every turn. But maybe I'll enjoy it."

"It probably is a terrible idea. And maybe we should absolutely not act on this...spark between us. Especially since you're the one who's utterly impossible. And yet..."

"And yet?" Susannah could barely whisper the words.

Tess answered with a forceful kiss that knocked the breath from Susannah's throat and her glass from her hand to the carpeted floor. She was vaguely aware of the splash of the remaining wine, but how could it register against the feeling of Tess's fingers running through her hair?

Susannah pulled her closer, kissing back for all she was worth. She couldn't remember the last time something had felt so intimate. The press of Tess's lips was firm and sure, and the flicker of her tongue was teasing. Even clutching at each other, it didn't seem to be close enough. They kissed, and kissed, and the bun in Susannah's hair was no match for Tess and her insistent fingers. Just thinking what she might do with them elsewhere sent a thrill through Susannah that made her body jolt in anticipation.

Tess made an appreciative sound when she got a proper hold on the cascade of blonde curls, wrapping them once around her hand to keep Susannah close and slipping the other beneath her thin grey sweater.

"We should be careful," Susannah said when they relented for a moment, her lips tingling and her breathing a little strained. "Not because of anyone seeing, which they can't anyway. I really don't care. It's just when you get all forceful, tugging on my hair and kissing me like that, well, I'm not sure my self-control is a match for that."

"So, you're saying stop short of getting us arrested?"

"Sure, let's go with that," Susannah agreed.

Then Tess was quite deliciously on her again, pinning her back against the cushions and treating them both to a series of long, lingering kisses. It took considerable self-restraint for Susannah not to hook her leg around Tess's hip. The limits of a public place were becoming more apparent, and there were so many soft surfaces just waiting for them back home.

Susannah didn't even register the ringing at first. It was just a background annoyance, no more than the buzz of an insect. Then Tess pulled away with real reluctance, and Susannah groaned.

"I'm firing whoever this is," Susannah said by way of apology. "Please hold that thought."

Summoning the last scraps of her composure, Susannah took a steadying breath and picked up the call.

Chapter 17

THEY DIDN'T SAY MUCH ON the drive back. A few times, quite innocently while changing gear, Tess's knuckles dragged against Susannah's thigh. It wasn't as if she needed to sit that close to the gears, and she didn't move any of the times it happened.

Tess rode out a fresh surge of relief every time Susannah stayed put, the sting of the first rejection almost soothed now by the flurry of kisses and the issues they'd talked out. One thing had been proven already—that the attraction between them certainly had the power to overcome any doubts and concerns. Maybe that was irresponsible, but to Tess it felt more like finally having all her choices back, and pursuing the one she wanted most of all.

"So..." Tess finally said when they were about halfway back to Hayleith. "Did Finn say how bad it is?"

Susannah snapped out of her reverie. "Hmm?"

"I asked if Finn gave you much detail. Is this just a stalling tactic, or can Robin really mess you up?"

"The solicitors are dealing with it." Susannah checked her phone again despite the lack of signal on this stretch. "They don't think the injunction will stand, but it can slow me down. It might also give the council a reason to deny me permission. That's the real stumbling block."

"That offer to take a hockey stick to her car still stands." Tess squeezed Susannah's leg. "And I'm sorry if all that back there was a distraction when you need to focus on other things."

"What? Oh no," Susannah said, leaning across to kiss Tess on the cheek. "No, this is one thing going right. I don't want you to think all I care about is business and money and—"

"I don't think that," Tess jumped in. "I've seen you with the horses, and I've heard all the things you've said about what you're trying to get done. You don't deserve this resistance, Suze."

"Oh, you think you've been promoted to nickname level, do you?" Susannah teased.

Tess enjoyed hearing the lightness creep back in. Keeping a vet practice afloat was stressful in some ways, but she couldn't imagine having all that responsibility every day. In Susannah's shoes, she might well have sold off the whole thing and retired young to a nice cottage in the south of France. That was what rich people did, wasn't it?

"Well if I'm not on those terms already, I'm happy to work my way up to them," Tess replied.

"You were making good progress. I really am sorry about the interruption."

"I know, I know."

"It's just there are things they can't do without me. I have to speak to the right people, sign some things, work out what comes next."

Tess took Susannah's hand.

"Hey, it's seriously fine. I was just putting the offer out there in the universe. We'll pick it up another time. At least I hope we will." Even when she was trying to sound confident and reassuring, Tess couldn't help but let a smidgen of doubt creep in. Rich, gorgeous, powerful women like Susannah just weren't supposed to fall for the local vet.

She let go of Susannah's hand to change gear again. This would have been a great time to drive an automatic. "Let's get you back to your office, so you can rain down hell on those who deserve it."

They drove on in comfortable silence, and Tess smiled when Susannah resettled her hand on Tess's thigh.

"You're back early." Margo walked into the staff room where Tess had just reunited with Waffles. "I thought you and Lady Muck would be out most of the day."

"She's going to take the horses at the farm, and we didn't get a chance to go to the second set." Tess scritched Waffles behind his ears until his back foot thumped on the floor in time with his tail. "More business for us, yay!"

"Yay?" Adam took off his lab coat as he joined them. "I don't think that's a word I've ever heard you say before."

"He has a point." Margo ran her hand unconsciously over her bump, which had started to show much more in recent weeks. "You look suspiciously chipper for someone who just spent hours with our most difficult client."

"You haven't been on the ketamine, have you? The party drugs are just for the animals, remember?" Adam asked, and luckily for him, he was joking.

Even so, Tess found that he wasn't quite as irritating as usual. "No, just out with a couple of fine horses, that's all. The younger one has some mild hip inflammation, so that's going to be the first job for us."

"For you," Margo replied. "I don't fancy a trip up to the stables. She probably keeps a stall for the staff to sleep in."

"She's not that bad," Tess started to protest, and too late she realised the trap that had been set.

"Aha!" Margo and Adam called out in unison.

"You do like her," Margo said, triumphant. "Pay up, Adam. I told you she got up to something at that night out."

"Now, wait a minute," Adam said. "Defending someone's reputation is no proof of anything. It's not like they were snogging behind the bike sheds or anything."

Tess wished more than anything that she didn't have the typical ginger's complexion. Any other skin tone and she might have been able to hide it, but she could feel the heat of a blush racing up her neck and over her cheeks.

"Oh-ho!" Margo was practically out of her chair at this development. "Theresa Claire Robinson, you've been holding out on us. There is gossip afoot, and you have been keeping it to yourself. Unacceptable!"

"Eh, not to get in the way of the sleepover bonding vibe here or anything," Adam said, "but aren't we a little concerned that we're talking about fooling around with our biggest meal ticket here? Midsummer Estate can seriously keep our lights on. You've already racked up a couple of thousand from the initial few visits and problems."

"Adam!" Margo scrunched up the paper from whatever she'd brought for lunch and tossed it at his head. It bounced right off his overly styled short hair and hit Tess on the shoulder instead. "Tess is our best friend. Her happiness matters more than money."

It was nice to hear that, although Tess suspected the enthusiasm was more about Margo still trying to make up for the lack of honesty around their going into partnership.

"There's not much to tell." Tess knelt beside Waffles and pulled him into a hug. "Yes, okay, fine. A little bit of kissing. Some talking. Way too many bloody interruptions, and that's about it."

"I didn't think you two got on." Adam sounded determined to be right about something. "Oh, wait, is it some kind of hate-sex thing?"

"Sorry to disturb your 'melting the ice queen' fantasies there, mate, but I've been getting to know the woman behind the fancy title, and she's not like all the rumours suggest. She isn't obsessed with power and screwing over the little guy. Susannah is..."

"Oh, Susannah, is it?"

"Shut up, Adam," Margo said. "Tess, you look really loved-up, girl."

"Let's not be throwing around l-words just yet, eh?" Tess wondered if she was ever going to stop blushing. "Please don't say anything to her, and if you could resist gossiping about it in the pub, I'd really appreciate it. You two didn't grow up in a small town, but you must know from living here how much pressure gossip puts on people. I just don't want to wreck this before it has a chance."

"You want to give it a proper go," Margo replied, coming around the table to pull Tess back to standing, then crushed her with a hug. "Of course. We'll do whatever you need. And, hey, don't forget you can just come and talk to me about any of this. It's not gossip when you're telling your best mate about the girl you like."

"Thank you." Tess exhaled. She never had this breathing space or support when she first met Caroline. It had all been so intense, Caroline insisting that relationship matters were totally private and not to be discussed with friends or family. Sometimes Tess wondered how she ever coped with that at all. "I promise, when there's anything to tell, you'll be my first port of call."

"Don't suppose you fancy dealing with my parrot appointment now that you're back?" Margo asked when their hug finally ended. "I'm not above bribing you with one of the brownies I made last night."

"Okay, but only for the brownie."

It was hardly a big deal when Tess hadn't heard from Susannah by bedtime. She certainly considered sending a text of her own, although they had only used their phones to talk work so far. Would that be pushing it? With the trouble that had landed earlier, it was hardly unreasonable that Susannah would be too busy or exhausted to initiate a chat. Tess turned in without giving into temptation, but she definitely had an unsettled night.

She was just out of the shower the next morning when she heard a knock at the door downstairs. Wrapped in her towel, she jogged down with some pointed mutterings about how the postman couldn't just leave things on the doorstep for her to pick up when they didn't fit through the door. Instead of Jerry the seventy-year-old postie, though, Tess opened the door a crack to reveal Susannah.

"Oh."

"Morning. Sorry for turning up unannounced. I'm...well, I'm sick of the sight of my phone but I needed to talk to you. And I wanted to get out of the house for a minute, and I just got in the car and..."

"Here you are," Tess finished for her. She opened the door the rest of the way.

"Come in. You caught me before getting dressed, though."

Susannah's gaze was scorching as she dragged it up and down Tess's towel-clad form. Most days Tess felt a little clumsy, awkward in her own skin. She was well aware that her fuller figure wasn't the type that graced magazine covers or television screens, but under Susannah's attention Tess felt her muscles flex and she stood just a little straighter. Even if, yes, she was blushing again.

"I brought coffee." Susannah held up a tray with two cups even though her eyes never left Tess. "Because I didn't want to throw off your morning too much. And yet..."

"I'd love to finish that thought," Tess replied, and it couldn't have been more accurate. "But I have a tough first appointment today, and I can't let the family down."

"Something sad, then." Susannah worked it out easily enough. "In that case, let me take a minute to boost your spirits. Wouldn't do to have our best vet feeling down all day."

She set the coffee on the kitchen table and reached for the bump in Tess's towel where it was tucked in to keep it in place. For a moment, her fingers just clutched at the white cotton, and Tess thought the whole thing was about to drop. Then Susannah used that grip to pull her closer, and her kiss was far hotter than Tess's knees knew what to do with. She almost lost her balance, but as soon as her head went back to a manageable level of spinning, Tess found herself naturally taking charge. She backed Susannah up against the fridge, her hand on the towel trapped between them as they made out.

"Sorry," Tess muttered against Susannah's lips when the kissing halted for a moment. "It's unbelievably tempting, but I've only got ten minutes. When I head up to my bedroom it's going to have to be alone."

"We could—"

"It is going to take way, way more than ten minutes for what I want to do with you. You're going to have to be patient, Suze."

Tess whispered the nickname against Susannah's ear before nipping at her earlobe, the perfect introduction to placing a trail of kisses down the elegant line of her throat. Their height difference didn't get in the way, but it was approaching dangerous territory for someone with only a towel to preserve her modesty.

Susannah whined softly when Tess stopped at the collar of her silky blouse, pulling away with a full step backwards to make the point. "I actually came to ask you something. Are you free tonight?"

"Short notice." Tess picked up her coffee. It was strong and hot and milky, her favourite combo.

Susannah peeled herself away from the fridge to pick up her espresso.

"But I don't have plans, as it happens," Tess finished.

"I need to make an appearance at a social thing tonight. I didn't even know about it until yesterday, but basically I need to get these council bigwigs on my side or else Robin can do my plans some very real damage. I'd prefer not to walk into the lion's den alone, honestly, but there's no pressure."

"Won't... I mean, that's really public. And you'll be there on work business."

"It's actually a fundraiser for the LGBTQ centre the council's opening. I figure—and I'm sorry for how cynical this sounds—but if they show up trying for diversity points and then I suggest that turning me down would look like discrimination... Although I really hate to play that card. I think I can convince them to back me without having to get to that level."

Susannah was almost rambling, and it seemed strange coming from her.

Tess was no fan of formal events, but she knew this was the perfect time to make an exception. "If anyone can convince them you're doing good things, it's you. I'll be there. Just give me an idea of what to wear and when you're picking me up."

Susannah grabbed her, and the kiss was short and sweet this time. "Thank you. Thank you. I promise it won't take the whole evening, and we'll have some fun too. Open bar, if nothing else."

"Okay, get going so I can get ready for work. Text me details later."

"I will. Really, Tess, this means a lot to me."

"You can show me how much later, but—"

"I'm gone, I'm gone." Susannah backed out of the kitchen. "And I'll be wearing a dress tonight that I swear you're going to enjoy."

That made it Tess's turn to groan in frustration. It was going to be a very long day.

Chapter 18

Susannah parked the Land Rover in the pub car park, figuring that it was easier than navigating the narrow road down by Tess's house.

Tess had been texting back and forth most of the afternoon, asking for more detail on what *formal* meant and what Susannah was wearing and if they had to coordinate. It was sweet, but Susannah had barely a minute to spare over each message. If her replies were abrupt, she'd have to hope for forgiveness, or the drive over was going to involve some grovelling on her part.

Perhaps she should have sent Finn to pick out something for Tess and take it round. This was a favour, after all, tentatively dating or not. Dresses and heels weren't really Tess's thing, it seemed, and Susannah appreciated that it was a pain for events such as these. Luckily, she didn't go to many.

God, she was exhausted. Her brain hadn't stopped for a second in two days. Why couldn't it have been over more of the kissing-in-pubs kind of thing and a lot less of the corporate skullduggery?

That thought had her both weary and distracted as she knocked on Tess's door for the second time that day. There was a long silence before the door slowly creaked open. Someone should really oil those hinges.

The sound was momentary distraction enough to pull Susannah's focus. When she looked back to Tess, she actually gasped at the sight before her. There was no little black dress in evidence, and that fluffy white towel of this morning had nothing on the sight that greeted Susannah.

"Listen, I got it for a costume thing a few years ago. Only, Caroline laughed at it, so I never did get to wear it."

Susannah just nodded, lost for words as she tried to catalogue each detail. There was the hair, for a start. Slicked back and pinned up in a discreet French twist, from the front, it passed as a much more masculine style.

Letting her gaze track downwards, Susannah could see that this was no novelty costume but rather a lovely piece of tailoring, from the slightly boxy shoulders to the cinched waist of the tuxedo jacket. Its silky lapels caught the last of the day's sunlight once Tess stepped forward from the doorway. The white shirt beneath was starched stiff, and Susannah thought it might make a pleasant scrunching sound if she grabbed it. The tapered black trousers give way to black kitten heels, a splash of femininity to complement the ruby lipstick and heavy, dark eyeliner that made Tess look bolder than usual.

It was a lot. The fact that Tess's lipstick matched Susannah's dress almost exactly was the icing on the cake.

"I can change," Tess blurted in the wake of Susannah's stunned silence. "Sorry, I just thought it might make for a cool effect, and I don't really have many dresses to choose from, so—"

"Don't." Susannah cleared her throat to take the strained sound out of her voice. "Don't you dare change. That is not coming off until I take it off later—are we clear?"

Tess grabbed the doorframe, seemingly bracing herself in response to Susannah's possessive growl of a comment. "Oh, so you like it, then?"

"Enough that you're in more danger of me marching you upstairs right now than you were in just your towel."

"But you need to go save your life's work," Tess pointed out. "And I want at least a couple of hours appreciating you in that dress. How high does that slit go, just out of interest?"

The way she was standing, the dress was showing mostly from the knee down. Susannah leaned forward, flexing her calf to keep balanced in a four-inch heel. The dress parted further, revealing that the slit went almost all the way up her thigh. "Will that do?"

"Oh yes." She looked a little punch-drunk, and it suited her. Tess noticed the car keys in Susannah's hand. "Wait, you're driving?"

"Long story involving the car not showing up. Don't worry. I can still have some fun. Especially if you're there."

"Then let's get going." Tess closed the door behind her. "Or we really might not make it there with all these clothes intact."

"Thank you again for doing this," Susannah said, startled when Tess came around to the driver's side and opened the door for her first. *How chivalrous.* "I know I said this was about work," she continued as Tess got into the passenger seat.

"I understand," Tess replied, her jaw working a little. "I can be just your regular gal pal until we're away from the crowds."

"No, no," Susannah held off on starting the engine, reaching across to touch Tess's cheek, turning her head slightly so they were looking at each other. "I'm done with hiding, Tess. My father is gone, Jimmy doesn't need my discretion, and you will be the envy of every man or woman at this event tonight. I want to walk in there with you on my arm, and I want to show you off."

"And that's not a problem for you? For the business? Because I am more than proud to be on your arm tonight, Lady Karlson. Just say the word, and I'm all yours."

"Good," Susannah denied herself the brief pleasure of a kiss. The build of anticipation would only make it sweeter. "Then let's go make our official debut."

Susannah wasn't expecting the flurry of photographers. It turned out that beyond the local paper and some bloggers, there was also a press contingent down from Edinburgh because a couple of senior politicians were in attendance, both from Holyrood and Westminster. She was more than used to the glad-handing, but having those bigwigs suck up attention might affect her access to the councillors she needed to secure votes from.

"You look like you're plotting," Tess said, bringing Susannah a glass of soda and lime along with her own whisky. "If it's a hit list, can we start with the barman who keeps calling this 'scotch'? It's like he doesn't know what side of the border we're on. The cheek of it."

"Oh, that definitely goes on my list." Susannah looked around the hotel ballroom, festooned with strands of sparkling fairy lights and dotted with huge bouquets. It was beautiful, almost romantic, but she couldn't help thinking they'd have raised more for charity if they had hired a village hall instead of blowing the budget of a mid-sized wedding.

"Found your targets yet?"

"No, but the last person in the world I wanted to see just walked in."

Tess followed Susannah's discreet nod back towards the ballroom entrance. At first glance it had just been the usual small sea of old white men in poorly-secured bow ties, but there was no mistaking when the sea parted and Susannah laid eyes on Robin.

Susannah had to concede that her sister-in-law was somewhat dressed for the occasion, although judging by the blue velvet dress with puffy sleeves, Robin seemed to think the occasion was Princess Diana's wedding.

"Will she make a scene?" Tess moved closer, slipping a protective arm around Susannah's waist before freezing with her hand an inch from the red silk covering Susannah's hip. "Because it's okay if this changes your plans about public dating."

"To hell with that." Susannah pushed Tess's hand into place and turned in her easy half-embrace to press against her front. It was almost a dance move.

"Are you going to kiss me?" Tess's face turned quite serious.

For a moment, Susannah couldn't hear the music or the muted chatter of the room. There was just that bubble for the two of them, Tess staring up at her with an unspoken challenge behind her question, the same challenge that a handful of other women had issued in one way or another over the years, a call for Susannah to be brave, to finally admit to herself, and everyone around her, who she was and what she wanted. It was, in every way that mattered, a moment of truth. And Susannah was exhausted from too many years of lying.

"Thought I might." With the simple act of a kiss, she finally laid the ghost of her parents' disapproval to rest, throwing it on a bonfire along with Robin's and that of anyone else who dared to dislike it. Susannah couldn't really get at Tess's hair in order to muss it up, but she could lay a hand on her cheek while drawing her in for a soft, slow, almost chaste kiss.

But there really wasn't anything chaste about the way Tess kissed. Her grip tightened momentarily, and Susannah's brain offered a vision of being hoisted up on the nearest table, glasses shattering as they were shoved roughly out of the way.

Those pleasant daydreams came to an end when Robin approached. She must have marched straight across the dance floor, which wasn't really populated yet despite the small band in the corner giving their very best take on ABBA's back catalogue. Clichéd perhaps, but worthy of some dancing all the same.

"And what kind of spectacle is this?" Robin's jewellery was practically rattling at her throat and at her ears. "If you think you can come here and embarrass my brother's memory by parading around some…some…"

"Woman?" Susannah filled in for her. "Robin Karlson, this is Dr Tess Robinson. Tess, this is the infamous Robin. I think she thought she'd have the councillors to herself tonight so she can continue her campaign of harassment against me."

Robin raised her hand to point at Susannah—one of those rude, stabbing gestures beloved of headmistresses and arguing drunks. Tess took a step forward, and Robin wheeled around to glare at her.

"Oh, no you bloody don't," Susannah warned, inserting herself between Robin and Tess like a human shield. "You lay a finger on Tess and you really will regret it."

"We'd prefer that nobody make a scene," Tess sounded every bit as capable of standing up for herself.

Robin wrinkled her nose, probably at the sound of Tess's broad Scottish accent, not a hint of poshness about it. Susannah tamped down an uneasy recollection of how many times she'd also made similar unsubtle judgements.

"I'm a valued supporter of this organisation," Robin said, although Susannah had it on good authority that Robin's so-called position as an ally began and ended with an occasional cheque to keep up appearances. Jonathan came scuttling across the room, just as if he had been summoned, dragging behind him a tall balding fellow who looked unsettlingly like Jimmy.

"Trouble here, Robin? Do you need anything?"

"No, Jonathan. If anyone is asked to leave due to making trouble tonight, it shan't be me," Robin replied with a haughty sniff. "You'd do well to go home and talk to your solicitors, Susannah. I'm sure when they're done gouging you they'll tell you I have a strong case and that it's really less trouble to step aside. Midsummer needs a suitable successor to its laird. James was so beloved."

"Jimmy was loved," Susannah agreed, and somewhere inside of her, the dam of propriety and the need to hide her feelings finally broke. "I know that because I was the one who was there when he got ill. Some of us only did monthly visits. Then to see what you've tried to do to his good name and mine, and to the estate's legacy? He'd be disgusted with you. Absolutely disgusted."

They were drawing attention now. Susannah had tried to keep her voice down, but their body language was giving them away. "My solicitors say you're the one with no case, and I've been indulging you because I thought it was grief all this time. Now I see you're just after the money, and you'll get that over my dead body."

"Listen, I don't know how you conned my brother for so long with your *arrangement*," Robin snapped. "But you don't deserve any of it. I was going to let you have that dreary pub of yours. Maybe it's time you got behind the bar and worked for a living. But I think now I'm going to include that in my claim. God knows my family paid for it."

Tess got fully between them then, not laying a finger on Robin but preventing her access to Susannah. "I think it's time you went to get a drink and rejoined your friends, if you even have any. Spin whatever lies you want, but you are not embarrassing Susannah any more than you already have. Another sniff of trouble, and I'll throw you out myself."

"When I want advice from the help, I'll ask for it," Robin replied.

There was a single crackling second when Susannah thought Tess might lose that ready temper of hers. She put a hand on Tess's arm, rubbing gently. "Let's go over here," she suggested as Robin strutted off towards the gaggle of inbred posers she arrived with, leaving Jonathan in her wake. "I just saw one of the councillors I need to turn, so I might be able to get her on board before Robin even knows she's here. And thank you, incidentally."

"For what?" Tess turned, her jaw set a little too stiffly and her brow furrowed, but she seemed to shake it off when Susannah gave her a promising look.

"The chivalry," Susannah answered. "She should never have spoken to you like that, though. I'll make her pay for that on top of everything else."

"You don't have to. She'll get hers." Tess adjusted her collar and the sleeves of her tuxedo jacket. It really was one hell of a look. "Now, let's go charm your councillors."

"You were amazing," Susannah said not for the first time. They were loitering at the driver's door of her car, because she liked being held in Tess's arms that way. It wasn't a particularly tight embrace, just arms wrapped around Susannah's lower back with Tess's hands resting high on her ass. "Really, I didn't know you could be that charming. I think at least one of those councillors was ready to propose."

"What can I say?" Tess looked pleased with herself, tucking a loose strand of hair behind Susannah's ear. "It's just a shame it's a long drive home, or we could crack the champagne and celebrate right now."

"I'm not counting my chickens just yet. Not until they actually vote on permission next week."

"Fair. We should head home. Not to rush you or anything but—"

Susannah couldn't resist stealing a proper kiss. They'd kept it strictly family-friendly all night since Robin had accosted them, and there was a certainty in the air that something more intimate was overdue.

Tess moved a hand behind Susannah's neck, holding her close, and Susannah revelled in the knowledge that they were absolutely going to sleep together tonight.

"Right, let's get going. Not to be too presumptuous, but your place or mine?" Susannah asked.

"I'd say yours has a bit more privacy," Tess said once she was in the passenger seat. "Unless the servants come barging in every morning?"

"I don't really live in *Downton Abbey*, you know."

"Good. Because that show makes me want to pass out copies of Marx and get the revolution underway."

"Yet here you are, compromising your principles for me." Susannah steered them towards the road home.

"Ah yes, principles. I remember those. Turns out they're no match for the sight of you in that dress. Seeing you all fired up for a fight didn't exactly hurt, either."

They didn't talk much on the way back. The roads outside weren't lit, and only the occasional oncoming set of headlights broke up the long stretches of darkness.

"I love driving at night," Susannah said. In a few minutes they'd reach the boundary of her land. "Especially around here. You can feel like you're the only one left in the world."

"There's something about it," Tess agreed. "We can't have too far to go now?"

As she asked the question, the Land Rover started to make a whining sound that didn't bode well at all. They'd turned onto one of the private roads on Midsummer's land, leaving the main road a way behind, hidden from sight by high hedges and the fact that the moon was barely a sliver through some fog.

"It'll be fine," Susannah said. The engine must have heard her because it ground to a halt with a horrible noise. "Ah. Fuck."

"I don't think I've heard you properly swear before," Tess said.

"Don't suppose your secret passion is fixing cars?" Susannah fumbled around in the glove compartment for a torch. It meant leaning across and inhaling the wood-smoke scent of Tess's cologne—altogether too tempting.

"You've mocked my car. Do I strike you as being one someone would take apart and rebuild from scratch?"

"Maybe with Lego," Susannah replied. "Sorry. Can't help myself."

A hissing sounded, and then wisps of smoke started to rise from the front of the car.

"Shit!" Tess squealed, the sound utterly at odds with her suave look. "Okay, so staying in the car isn't an option. You do know roughly where we are, right?"

"We can follow the road back or wait for someone to pass and pick us up," Susannah said as they slammed the doors shut and she pocketed the keys. Flicking the torch on, she was dismayed to see that it was already dim. "Even if I could walk to the house or the village in these shoes, this light isn't going to get us across the fields. Not far enough."

An ominous rumble sounds overhead.

"Oh, that better not be thunder," Susannah tried not to groan. Pulling her phone out, she offered a silent prayer for even one bar of signal.

Nothing. A glance at Tess confirmed the same for her.

"Okay, let's reassess," Tess said, not entirely succeeding at hiding her panic. "Where is the nearest shelter you can think of? From there we can try phones and roads and other things again, but I don't think that rain is far off."

"We should be near one of the unoccupied tenant farms." She hoped her internal compass wasn't far off. She was going to have take this situation—

and Tess—in hand. Raiding the boot for supplies, she unearthed a blanket and some bottled water, among other things. A start. "I don't think much of it is still standing, though. We'll freeze if we stay with the car, and I'm not wild about that smoke coming from the engine."

"It should be fine with the engine off," Tess said. "Although when it comes to smoke and petrol, it's definitely a 'less is more' sort of situation. I don't think I could relax."

The rain started then, fat drops falling from the dark sky above.

"Which way?" Tess asked. "Cover is the main thing; we'll work out the rest."

Susannah got her bearings, and they started to jog down the road. If only she'd thought to keep boots in the car. Tess steadied her each time the heels made her stumble.

"There!" Susannah picked out the stone building with a wave of the torch. "Just in time too."

The rain was coming down harder then, reducing what little visibility they had. Just as the first fork of lightning split the sky, they reached what looked like an abandoned barn.

"Hurry!" Tess shouted over the rain.

It was going to have to do.

Chapter 19

THIS WAS NOT THE NIGHT Tess signed up for, that was for damn sure.

Not that she could quite bring herself to mind, not when they were catching their breath in a dry, solid sort of building, their clothes damp from the rain but not that cold, thanks to the stormy conditions. At least now they were sheltered from what sounded like one hell of a storm.

Susannah's chest rose and fell sharply, bent over in her formal red dress.

"What is this place?" Tess asked, trying not to stare.

"It's a bothy. Sort of a bunk house for farmhands or passing campers. I forgot about it. I thought we'd have to go farther to hit the farm, which we probably would."

"I'm okay here for now if you are?" Tess walked around, not that there was much to explore. The ground floor was fairly flat, with odd stalks of hay withered here and there. There was an old camping stove with a gas canister next to it, a broken hiking pole, and a door leading to some kind of outhouse area. Better than nothing.

"I'm sorry," Susannah said, keeping close so that the torch lit the way for both of them. "That car has never given me a moment's trouble before. When the weather eases off, we can try and get some phone signal, because I've got nothing here."

"At least we're safe inside," Tess replied, pulling out her phone. Wanting to preserve some of Susannah's torch, she lit up the torch app. It illuminated a sturdy ladder leading up into a hole in the ceiling. "Loft space?"

"Probably where the bunks are," Susannah said. "If anything's left of them at this point. Let's go up the ladder and have a look around. It can only be more comfortable than all this open space."

Tess nodded and picked up the tiny stove. She shook the canister to make sure it had gas. "Right."

Susannah took her shoes off and headed up the ladder, followed by Tess. It was surprisingly well looked after. No leaks in the ceiling, but enough light through small gaps in the walls to make it much less dark inside. A few pallets were laid out, straw-stuffed mattresses with sacks on top of them. It couldn't have been that long since the place was last used.

Tess took a seat on the biggest "bed", kicking off her shoes and setting up the stove. A couple of minutes later, they had some light and heat, however long it would last.

"It's good you grabbed a few things before we left the car," Tess said.

Susannah came to settle beside her, dropping her supplies. There was a blanket, which Tess put on the mattress beside them. A large bottle of water. A couple of energy bars and an old coat rounded out the collection.

"It wasn't stupid to walk away from the car, was it?" Tess asked.

"Not at all. We had to get out of it, and hopefully with everything turned off it won't get any worse. These emergency provisions aren't great, though." She frowned. "This wasn't the hospitality I had in mind for you tonight."

"Hey, hey," Tess reached for Susannah's hand. "This could happen to anyone. Shame about our shoes, but we'll live."

"I had plans," Susannah replied. "Big plans that I promise you we would both enjoy very much."

"What a coincidence, because I fully intended on taking you straight to bed." Tess was trying to keep up, but when it came to seduction, Susannah already had her at a disadvantage. Just one raking glance, a faint flicker of tongue over those lips, and Tess was entirely malleable, ready for Susannah to sculpt and mould her at will.

"I admire your confidence in thinking we'd get that far. My money was on the first soft surface we came to." Susannah leaned closer, her eyes focused on Tess's lips.

"Oh really?"

"Doesn't even need to be that soft."

Susannah reached out between them and pressed the improvised mattress. "Hmm. Dry. Firm. Add a blanket and this is just perfect for right now, wouldn't you say?" Her eyebrow lifted.

That simple gesture came for Tess like a ton of bricks. This wasn't casual flirting anymore, or some hasty but enjoyable kisses. They were inches apart, and here was Susannah, in all her Lady Karlson finery, suggesting she shove Tess down right there and have her wicked way.

The very idea sent a tidal wave of want crashing through Tess's body. The dull throb of wanting became a constant, arching need that seemed to keep drawing their bodies together. With her long, careful fingers, Susannah reached out and undid her bow tie, then left it to dangle around her neck. She twisted the first button on Tess's dress shirt, freeing it. Susannah moved right down to the next button. And the one after that.

As soon as she ran out of buttons, Susannah pulled Tess into the kind of kiss that left zero ambiguity about her intentions. At one point in the meeting of lips and tongues, one of them actually whimpered. Tess wasn't sure if it was her.

The primitive surroundings didn't dampen their need for each other one bit. Any cold in the air was chased off by the heat generated between them, and the glow of the stove was a safe distance from where they were slowly becoming entangled with each other.

Tess ran her hand up Susannah's thigh, bared by the slit in her dress. The silky skin seemed to go on forever, the silk of the dress never presenting any kind of barrier until the last possible inch. Under her palm, the toned muscles of Susannah's leg flexed and jumped. Those countless days in the saddle had toned her body into a living sculpture, an absolute work of art.

Susannah took full advantage of that part in the fabric to get one long leg wrapped around Tess.

The dress at Susannah's shoulders gave way at the slightest tug. That let Tess explore her more fully, with open-mouthed kisses from that strong jawline to the elegant, almost fragile hollows at Susannah's neck and collarbones. Her skin was impossibly soft, whether from expensive lotions or just genetic luck; Tess couldn't bring herself to care. All she knew was that Susannah felt perfect against her lips, something that had been true since their very first kiss.

"God, I've wanted you all night," Susannah said, grabbing the collar of Tess's shirt. "At one point I thought I was just going to rip the buttons right off and have my way with you there and then."

"If anything, it's a miracle we made it through the evening without my hand under this dress," Tess said. "It's practically an engraved invitation to everywhere I've been dying to touch you. Which I think is exactly why you wore it, isn't it?"

To think of Susannah, with her designer wardrobe existing like an arsenal for her to choose from, picking out a dress just to render Tess incoherent with lust, was more than Tess could have hoped for.

Susannah's smirk was unmistakable as Tess cupped her left breast through the fabric of her dress. Rubbing a thumb across the already stiff nipple, Tess delighted in the moan that bubbled up from Susannah's throat. It seemed as if she was going to be every bit as vocal in this as she was in the rest of her life, and Tess couldn't wait to hear that.

"I wore it to make sure you appreciated just what you were in for tonight. Just like you were trying to kill me with the whole soft-butch James Bond thing."

"And...you like that," Tess said, her voice knowing. "You want me to want to please you."

"Oh, very good. Gold star for the good doctor."

Tess responded with another searing kiss, pushing Susannah down until she was flat on her back. Another tug at the dress bared more of her body, down to the top edge of her strapless bra. With one leg exposed, the rest of the dress was barely a barrier, but Tess took her time shimmying the soft material down to expose inch after inch of lightly tanned skin.

"Gorgeous," Tess said, finally setting the dress aside. She rocked back on her heels and drank in every detail of the sight before her. It took a moment to remind herself to breathe, so struck was she by Susannah starting to come undone. Tess's impatience to touch every part of her spiked. She quickly dispatched her jacket onto their growing pile of clothes. Tess's shirt that Susannah had unbuttoned hung open, halfway off her shoulders.

The hunger in the way Susannah watched was scorching, but it was nothing compared to the sensation of her hands tracing Tess's curves as they exposed themselves.

Her bra was more substantial than Susannah's, but then it had quite a lot to carry. Susannah reached up to tease a finger along the lace edge of each cup, her smile downright greedy, and Tess gasped. Each pattern Susannah traced seemed calculated to drive Tess out of her mind, but supporting herself on her forearms, she forced herself to lean forward and pressed Susannah down on the bed of hay. Her last threads of self-control were fraying as Susannah shifted under her, forcing more contact between them. This was the all-powerful woman who always got what she wanted, and every sensitive part of Tess was revelling in remembering just why. This was usually the point where Tess would be self-conscious about the extra pounds she was carrying, but the heat of Susannah's gaze left no room for doubt or fear.

At another time, Tess might have lingered, might have teased for minutes that felt like hours, but at the first sign of dallying, Susannah gripped her shoulders, blunt nails pressing into the skin.

Tess unhooked Susannah's bra and then wrenched the underwear down her legs, leaving her naked. If she'd been a work of art before, now Susannah was fantasy made flesh, her hips canted and her legs spread in anticipation, everything in her pose an invitation to more. If she wasn't careful, Tess could get lost in wanting something this much, but fuck, was she ever done with being careful. Tess landed a series of determined kisses on her hipbones.

"Oh, straight to the point," Susannah rasped. "You must like what you see."

"Do you want me to take my time?" Tess paused long enough to ask. She was on her knees now, the floorboards creaking beneath her. "Because I can take all night over this. All. Night."

Susannah's answer was tangling the fingers of one hand in Tess's hair and tugging with fierce intent. The lady apparently did not want to be kept waiting.

"So I'll get on with it, then," Tess said.

Susannah's grip only tightened as Tess set about the task with more enthusiasm than she could ever remember having before. She did love going down on a woman, maybe because taste was an underrated part of the experience, but this was something else entirely. When it came to Susannah, Tess wanted to do everything, and she wanted to do it as many times as humanly possible.

Despite the lack of foreplay that Tess would usually lavish on a lover, Susannah was already slick beneath the first determined swipes of Tess's tongue, and so she dragged her blunt fingernails down the insides of Susannah's thighs, which parted readily to welcome her between them.

Tess turned the full pressure of her licking toward Susannah's clit, stiff in anticipation of the contact.

"Oh God!" Susannah gasped.

Tess continued the relentless pace. There was still so much more of Susannah she wanted to touch and taste, but Susannah was already squirming under her touch.

They'd been building up to this all night, and they desperately needed a release. The more Tess twisted and twirled her tongue, alternating flicks of the tip with broad flat strokes, the more Susannah unravelled.

Susannah's thigh muscles tensed and then trembled, the arch of her hips pushing her harder against Tess's mouth. Her orgasm resulted in a half shout, and Susannah's hand slapped against the mattress until straw and dust flew up in the air.

It wasn't until she was quaking through her second orgasm that Tess started to let up. Susannah tried to admonish her, but all that came out was a sort of strangled cry.

Tess wiped her mouth with the back of her hand, smearing a little on the sleeve of her open shirt, enjoying the way Susannah's eyes darkened at the sight. "You look amazing like this." Tess was still on her knees. "Like I'm worshipping at your shrine."

"Careful," Susannah replied, recovering her voice. "I could get used to that sort of devotion. Still, I haven't had my turn yet, have I, *Tess*?"

Tess swallowed.

Susannah grabbed the edges of Tess's shirt and pulled her down into a confident kiss, seemingly only spurred on by tasting herself on Tess's lips. Leveraging with her knee, Susannah rolled them over. Backlit by the beams of moonlight as she leaned over Tess, the woman looked like a goddess.

"I'm going to enjoy this," Susannah announced.

Seconds later, Tess was in complete agreement.

Chapter 20

"Morning," Susannah said, wide awake and running a determined finger along Tess's bare collarbone.

Tess gave a soft grunt and tried to turn away from her.

The light was streaming in through the gaps in the walls around them, like dozens of little lasers. While the air was crisp and fresh from the storm, it was also very chilly. Even in their mostly dry clothes and pressed against one another, they were not generating enough heat to fight that off anymore.

"No."

"No? I tell you it's morning, and you're what…just refusing to accept it?"

"Mmff," Tess replied, trying to turn on the mattress and getting poked in the cheek by errant straw. She still didn't open her eyes. "Okay, this is not my bed."

"There's that brilliant investigative mind I rely on to diagnose my horses."

"Hey!" Tess pushed herself up to sitting. With her underwear still missing in action, she was wearing her unbuttoned shirt inside out and her dress trousers unzipped but basically in place. "Fuck a doodle do, it's cold."

"Well, this camping trip wasn't exactly planned, so we're low on thermal sleeping bags. It's probably a good excuse to get up and start heading back to civilisation."

"Fair, fair," Tess agreed. She stretched her arms up above her head, rolling her neck with a series of cracks and relieved-sounding groans.

Susannah did not hide her stare at the way it thrust her breasts out front and centre.

"Oh, and hey. Morning to you." Tess leaned over to kiss Susannah—a gentle press of lips.

Despite their bedraggled appearance—Susannah didn't even want to think about what her hair might be doing—it was hard to remember seeing anyone more beautiful. It was a word that had been missing from Susannah's life too long. "We'll go back and check on the car, then head for the road and grab whoever's passing. It's barely six," she said, checking her watch. "So it shouldn't mess up the day or anything."

Once they had made themselves as presentable as they could and had tidied up, they headed back to the Land Rover. Objectively, Susannah knew that cars couldn't sulk, but the poor broken lump of thing definitely had that energy.

"Want to give it a try?" Tess asked. "Sometimes just letting it cool down is enough."

The car resolutely refused to start, sounding angrier with each attempt.

"Okay, let's head for the main road, then," Tess said. "Remind me why I didn't wear flats with a suit?"

"Because you were toying with gender roles as well as my libido?" Susannah liked this easy morning-after teasing. It could have been awkward. Instead she held out her hand for Tess to take, and they fell into a gentle rhythm with as they walked.

Tess had relaxed her slicked-back hair, her regular ponytail back in place.

"The low heels aren't as bad as these, at least," Susannah added.

Tess took an appreciative look at Susannah's black leather high heels, seeming just as impressed as last night. "I can offer you a piggyback."

"After a night on that improvised bed? No chance. I'm not being held responsible for sending you to the osteopath."

"Sure about that?" Tess tugged Susannah close enough to kiss again. "Because I seem to remember you liked it when I really put my back into it last night. You're more than worth a bit of morning-after stiffness."

"Okay, Casanova," Susannah said. "Although I confess I'm looking forward to what you were promising about that strap-on."

Tess just about choked.

Susannah smirked. "Come on, it's not so far now. We can see where we're going."

They only had to wait fifteen minutes before they came across Dave and flagged him down. Susannah was glad to see a friendly face. The last thing she wanted was awkward silence with a complete stranger.

"Hello, hello." Dave brought his truck to a stop right by them. "Did I miss an all-night rave?"

"Dawidek, you're not funny." Susannah gestured for Tess to get in first. Luckily these huge sturdy farm trucks fit three in the front seat, because every inch of the back and the flatbed was crammed with crates and sacks of produce. "But are we going to make you late for a market day?"

"No, I'm always early. I'll take you back to ours, and Finn will take you the rest of the way."

Susannah clambered in after Tess and leaned back against the seat with a sigh. Despite her early morning bravado, she was aching all over, particularly in places that hadn't seen such a vigorous workout lately. It was going to make gym time for the rest of the week even tougher than normal.

"Thanks for this," Tess said once they were in motion. "Let's see when we get signal again. Margo should have kept Waffles overnight when I didn't come back for him."

"Did you, uh," Susannah started to ask, giving Dave a warning glance as she turned to address Tess. He looked away with a grin. "Did you mention you might be out overnight?"

There was that blush again. "Yeah, well. I didn't rule it out, at least."

Susannah nudged Tess with her elbow, and they shared a sly, secret smile. It chased away the headache that had settled in behind her eyebrows. She rested her hand on Tess's thigh, an experiment of sorts, and when nobody reacted, Susannah felt the last of her stress lift from her shoulders.

Dave dropped them at the farmhouse gate and departed with a quick handbrake turn and a cheery wave. They'd clearly made him late, but he was too polite to say so.

Susannah made a mental note to send a bottle of something nice home with Finn for him.

"Before we interrupt Finn's morning," Tess said, letting go of Susannah's hand, "I just want you to know there's no pressure on this, not from me. I know we basically went public last night, but I also know what a big deal that was for you. I know it's early days, so I understand if you're waiting to see how it goes."

"Hayleith has a way of finding things out whether you want them to or not."

"Even so. I don't want to be the cause of any more stress. That said, I will always be extremely proud to have you on my arm, whether it's some charity ball or just picking up a croissant from Joan."

Susannah considered that for a moment, looking at the cute farmhouse in front of them. She hadn't been around here since Jimmy passed away, always too busy for excursions when Finn was already right there at Midsummer.

She saw now that the reason had been something else, an avoidance of happy couples in their adorable, normal-sized homes. Today that didn't seem all that bad. "Oh no, you won't get rid of me that easily, Tess. This thing between us is going somewhere good. Right now, though, we're only going as far as knocking on that door so Finn can take me home for a shower and work. On the way, we can drop you off so you can complete your walk of shame down Main Street, if that's out and proud enough for you?"

"Suze, I'm not—"

"I know, I know." Susannah kissed Tess as sweetly as she could, lingering for the sensation of those soft lips against her own. "But I am. Proud, I mean. I liked being out with you last night, so we should probably do that again. With better sleeping arrangements."

They were interrupted by the front door opening. Finn stood there, toothbrush in hand. "Are you two ever coming in? Or do you need a bit longer to come up with a cover story for how Dave found you all rumpled in a field?"

"No cover story," Susannah said, leading Tess indoors. "Car broke down, lots of rain, sheltered in a bothy overnight. That about covers it."

"You forgot the part where you clearly had lots of sex," Finn replied before disappearing back in the direction of the bathroom, so Susannah didn't get to register even mock offence. "Help yourselves to coffee—there's a pot by the cooker!"

Tess almost shoulder-charged Susannah out of the way to get there first.

"What happened to chivalry?" Susannah asked, trying very hard not to pout.

"Look, I'm pouring two," Tess said in her defence. "But that's pure instinct. Nobody gets between me and a reliable source of caffeine. You have straw in your hair, in case you were wondering."

Finn returned then, watching with the unabashed delight on their face usually reserved for talking about old episodes of *Buffy* or the merits of bow ties. "You can use the bathroom to clean up, if you'd like. There are spare towels and toothbrushes in the cupboard outside it. I'll be ready in ten or so? We'll be early, but it sounds like I have a lot to catch up on."

Susannah seized the opportunity for a moment alone and commandeered the bathroom, ignoring whatever Tess and Finn started chattering about as she closed the door. A long, painful look in the mirror confirmed the unscheduled night of roughing it had taken a toll. Raccoon eyes from the mascara, tousled knots of hair that were going to take a professional to sort out, and a rip across the top layer of her dress, the gauzy material parted like, well...

And yet she was still smiling.

A quick run through of her ablutions had her feeling more presentable.

Finn knocked and offered up a clean tracksuit that had to be Dave's. Like a low-budget Sporty Spice, Susannah rejoined the fray, rolling her eyes at Tess checking her out.

"Have you got a bag for this dress?" Susannah held the shredded garment up. "You know what? On second thought, straight to the incinerator. It's already torn, and I am not looking too closely for stains."

"You can't do that!" Tess said. "That's a bit decadent, isn't it?"

"As much as I'd like a souvenir, I think that's about ready to be condemned. I promise I put most things in the wash like a normal person."

"Or she sends me to get it dry-cleaned, at least," Finn said with just a hint of reproach, more than used to the turnover in Susannah's wardrobe. "Tess, would you like anything?"

"No, my ensemble's a bit more comfortable, thanks. Plus without it, how will anyone know to have a good gossip?"

"Fair point."

"I will take a quick turn in the bathroom, though." Tess passed with a quick pat of Susannah's bottom through the nylon tracksuit.

Finn waited until they were alone before half-collapsing with an "oh my Gooooooood" that seemed to go on for a full minute. "I cannot believe you went from 'Oh, I might eventually consider properly dating' to hooking up with the village's newest dyketastic hottie in the space of, what, three weeks?"

"I'm not keeping count," Susannah replied, but she laughed all the same. "I knew I could rely on you to have a calm and measured reaction, so thanks for that."

"Is this something real? Or are you just getting it out of your system? Because she looks pretty smitten."

"Real enough that I'm not sure how to answer that, not just yet. But what can I say? Must be my charm. We did run into my darling sister-in-law, though. Can you pull the deeds for the pub today just to make sure everything's watertight on that front?"

"Why does she care about the Thistle?" Finn gathered the empty coffee cups and stacked the dishwasher.

"Spite, mostly."

"She'll stick her horrible nose anywhere, that one. I'll just be glad when she stops calling every day."

"She has a cheek playing ally of the year at events like last night when her first petty instinct when she doesn't get her way is to misgender you." Susannah felt the rage relight inside her like someone had just struck a match—an especially big match hovering over a whole lake of petrol. "I will make sure to settle that score with her too, Finn. She won't get away with it."

"Like I said, it doesn't really bother me. Not from ignorant old sods like her, anyway. Wouldn't give her the satisfaction. Just make sure she doesn't get a penny, and I'll be happy."

"Oh, I will. Plus I think I got my council votes for real this time, thanks to Tess charming the socks off half the committee. You should have seen her. We're on track at last. You're going to have a whole army of minions to boss around at this rate."

"Just what I wanted. Oh, Babs left a message last night. Something about being away Thursday when the drayman is coming to stock up on all the big booze orders? I'll sort it out with her; I can always go down early."

"Or see if the Andersen lad will sleep over and do it after his shift. I'll pay him for the whole time."

"Cool, yeah."

Tess rejoined them, looking much fresher. "Back in work mode already? You really are a machine, woman."

"She is," Finn confirmed. "You two ready for a drive, then? Get you back in plenty of time for work, Doc."

"Let's go," Susannah said.

Tess rewarded her with a minty-fresh kiss.

The council chambers were housed in one of the grandest buildings in the county. The marble floors and wood-panelled walls would be just as suitable for a grand old university or maybe even a minor palace. They were also cold, draughty, and completely lacking in any kind of comfortable seating. Susannah and Finn waited outside the committee hearing room on the world's most rigid leather-topped bench seat.

"Feels like court." Susannah shuddered. "I suppose it does determine my future in a similar way."

"Hmm?" Finn was distracted by their phone. "Babs says the Andersen boy can't do the early deliveries. I'd go myself, but I have to be in Edinburgh by eight. I'll just tell her to skip a week and make do with what she has."

"No, we're not having the pub run out of booze." Susannah halted mid-thought at the sight of Robin approaching them, back in one of her favoured Miss Trunchbull ensembles of military-grade tweed skirt suit. "In fact, tell Babs that as she's such a valued member of staff, she should go off tonight without a worry. I'll stay over myself and be there for the drayman."

"Turning to bar work as I suggested?" Robin asked, all faux politeness as Jonathan, behind her, glared at his tablet and avoided eye contact with Finn and Susannah. "Probably wise to do some career planning."

"Lady Karlson?" The heavy wooden door opened. A small, balding man stuck his head out. "You wanted to know when we'd be turning to your application?"

"Thank you." Susannah gathered her coat and handbag and strode off before Robin could make a comment.

Ushering Finn in front of her, Susannah made sure to close the door right in Robin's face. Win or lose, this was still nothing to do with her. Not yet and not ever, if Susannah had anything to do with it.

Chapter 21

Tess wasn't sure what actually woke her.

The huge crashing sound, like a tree snapping in two, was certainly a contender. The cloying, clinging stink of smoke was another; she had always been sensitive to it. Last but not least, the garish light that flickered and grew brighter by the second might have been enough to disturb her well-earned rest, but her brain, along with the rest of her aching limbs, still felt sluggish and eager to return to bed. It was only when she dragged herself to the window and saw that the building across the quaint little courtyard was on fire that the adrenalin finally kicked in.

"The pub!" she gasped to no one in particular, which was hardly unusual, but where was Waffles? At the first sign of danger, he usually applied himself to Tess like a giant fluffy bandage, ready to protect her from anything.

She ran downstairs in mismatched pyjamas and almost overbalanced, but the brief wobble helped her catch sight of a pale yellow tail sticking out from under the dinner table.

"Waffles?"

He had never ignored her calls, save for a time or two when he got too enthusiastic about chasing a squirrel.

Tess glanced back at the flames, wondering why the hell she couldn't hear sirens or see blue flashing lights yet. "Here, boy," she coaxed, lifting the tablecloth to see him trembling and trying to press himself down through the floorboards. "It's okay, we're okay."

Her first instinct was to sit and soothe him, maybe root around in her bag for something mild to calm him down. Only in that moment she remembered what her sleep-addled brain had been trying to piece together for the past minute or two.

Susannah was sleeping over at the pub.

Something about Babs having the day off and the drayman and something else that had been lost in the noise of winning the council vote yesterday.

Tess was scrabbling back to her feet after what she hoped was a reassuring enough pat for her poor scared pup. Rushing to the front door, she shoved her bare feet into wellies and yanked her parka on at the same time. Fumbling, she did what she should have done on first waking and dialled 999.

She barreled out of the door without actually opening it properly, and that was definitely going to leave her with a bruised shoulder. Tess couldn't feel it. She just had to get over there.

Still no lights. No sirens. On the main road, curtains were twitching, and a door or two was opening, drawn out into the middle of the night like Tess had been. Tess wound her way through the sturdy wooden tables of the beer garden, getting as close as dared to the pub's back entrance.

The first shout went up.

Looking around, she saw Adam stumbling into view, in weirdly formal pyjamas that made him look like a younger Stephen Fry. His hair was sticking up in all directions. As he approached Tess, he ended a call on the phone he was clutching.

"What the hell are you doing?" he shouted at her.

The smoke was getting thicker now, she was so close. The heat was already making sweat prickle along Tess's hairline.

"We have to...Susannah!" She pointed to the burning building. Her brain was racing, but Tess's mouth couldn't keep up. She kicked at the ground with her wellies, frustrated by her lack of words.

"No, we have to wait for the fire brigade. I've called 999; so has everyone on the street, probably. Get back from there, Tess!" He ran toward her, waving her away, concern and fear etched in his features.

Tess saw it clear as day how this would play out. Everyone standing around, wringing their hands, worrying about risk. Meanwhile, a fire engine from God knew how far away was winding its way down the endless country roads to reach their little outpost.

"Going in!" Tess shouted back. Before Adam could do a damn thing about it, she shouldered the back door. The flimsy lock gave on the second shove.

Thank you, adrenalin.

It was already hard to breathe. Her chest was tight, her heart was hammering. Pure terror too, but Tess had always been more fight than flight, even when it was the stupidest thing she could do.

The heat and roar of the flames was coming from the main pub lounge, and Tess didn't want to investigate any further. The faint sound of a smoke alarm was going off in there, but as she moved towards the corridor that led to the bedrooms upstairs, the lack of alarms screeching or beeping was painfully apparent. Thank God she'd been around here to see Babs in the back area before, or the entire layout would be unknown to her.

Visibility was poor. Tess didn't dare try to switch on lights. She couldn't remember why it was a bad idea, but she knew that it was.

Up the stairs, rooms sat on either side of the short hallway.

Tess nudged the first door all the way open but found it empty.

She coughed. *Fucking smoke.*

The next door was a bathroom, and she grabbed the hand towel from the rail, quickly soaking it and wringing it out. That gave her some relief over her nose and mouth.

Dropping on all fours, she crawled to keep her head out of the swirling smoke, and felt her way along to the next door.

Bingo! There was a double bed with someone under the covers. Tess practically threw herself at the shape.

"Susannah! Suze!"

The lump didn't respond, just groaned a little.

Tess took in the sleep mask, the earplugs. There was a little bottle of something on the nightstand. *Shit.* Apparently Susannah took something to help her sleep. Fantastic.

Still no lights or sirens from outside. The smoke was getting thicker and lower. It was in her face now even when she hunched over.

This couldn't wait.

It had been a while since Tess had been to the gym. Walking Waffles was her daily workout, so when she grabbed Susannah, clad in dark silky pyjamas, lifting her turned out to be a whole new problem. Those long legs were a menace, and everything about Susannah seemed to be willfully floppy as Tess tried to leverage her off the mattress and into a fireman's lift.

In the end, sheer panic did most of the lifting, and Tess just had to hold her in place as best she could, the damn slippery material of Susannah's pyjamas only making it harder.

Moving was difficult. Tess was already out of breath, and Susannah's dead weight over her shoulders made keeping low much harder. Opting for speed over ducking down, Tess headed back to the door.

Smoke everywhere. *Shit. Which way are the stairs?* Tess turned, facing the door to get her bearings. To her right. That was it.

Susannah started to wriggle but Tess held on tighter. Even if she was waking up, this was no time to try and explain the situation to a groggy woman.

The roar of the fire was louder. Wood was splintering. Glass smashing. Tess took a step. Then the next.

Step. Step.

She wanted to cough so badly, it was like her throat was itching on the inside, but that was a bad idea. If she started coughing, it would only get harder to move. To think. To get out.

Halfway down the stairs, Susannah started to struggle, coming to. Tess shouted at Susannah to help her wake. When she finally gained consciousness, slipping from the clumsy over-shoulder hold under her own steam, Tess began dragging her, one insistent arm around her torso, down the rest of the steps.

Tess couldn't tell which of the doors downstairs was safe to open. The pub itself was a lost cause. She turned, pulling Susannah with her. There was no chance of going back the way she came in; that door had thicker smoke pouring through it.

"Which way?" she yelled against Susannah's ear, hoping she was rallying enough to have some kind of instinct.

Susannah lurched towards one of the doors. Tess moved with her.

It was the back room. Babs's living room. They staggered through it, both now on their knees by halfway. Tess looked around.

A door. A window. Anything?

Tess saw the heavy grey fire-exit door like a mirage through the smoke, a faint glow of green above it. Thank everything holy and not for whatever health and safety law made those fluorescent signs mandatory, because Tess could barely see a foot in front of her.

She threw herself at the door. The bar across it was pressed in by Susannah's shoulder as Tess yanked her towards it.

It opened. It was open, and they were out.

Stumbling, Tess made it as far as she could until her momentum finally gave out.

They were in the car park. There were voices, other hands lifting Susannah and letting Tess slump to her knees. Then, finally, she let the coughing come. Heavy barks squeezed her chest and shook her body. She hacked and hacked until she could breathe again, wondering how she hadn't passed out.

Adam was tending to Susannah. That was good. Adam was a sensible guy. Did all his first aid qualifications. Put the certificates on the wall. He was kneeling beside her and talking to her.

Someone passed Tess a bottle of water, and her gulps were punctuated by more coughing.

Tess crawled over to check on Susannah, but she was in the recovery position, eyes closed.

Tess's panic rose.

No, she was definitely breathing! Chest rise, chest fall.

Tess pressed her fingers to Susannah's neck and yes! That was her pulse. Not fast or strong enough, but there.

Adam was talking, but Tess couldn't hear him.

Maybe Susannah couldn't either.

The blue lights came at last. Bells ringing, sirens screaming. Chaos in the shape of a big red truck. Behind it, higher and reedier in pitch, came the ambulance. Help was here.

Tess had done enough, and now they were going to take over. She was crying—or was it just the smoke irritating her eyes? She lay on her side, facing Susannah.

Tess didn't care what the madding crowd thought when she reached out to stroke Susanna's soot-stained cheek. "They're coming. So don't you even think about not being okay. You got out, that's all that matters. And you promised me that once you got this pub issue sorted that we'd go out and celebrate your yes vote. You owe me a party, Lady Karlson. Don't you forget that."

Then the paramedics were suddenly there with their neon jackets and their latex-coated, capable hands.

Tess felt the last of her adrenalin wearing off and just let herself become pliable. She answered their questions and let them shine lights and prod things. Then there was a mask over her mouth and nose. Horrid, rubbery thing. Felt clammy, like someone else just had it on. Then she took a deep breath for what seemed like the first time in hours. Well. Much better.

"We're going to take you both to the hospital," the tall paramedic was saying, steering her to the waiting ambulance. No, there were two ambulances.

"I want to go with her!" Tess cried out, or tried to. The effort of saying it felt like a dozen knives dragged across the inside of her throat.

Susannah was on a stretcher and already being loaded into one of the ambulances.

"No room, and they have to monitor her on the journey," the paramedic replied. "Come on. The sooner you get in, the sooner you can see your friend again."

Tess didn't bother to correct him. She wasn't sure what she'd be correcting. She climbed up the vehicle's steps and took her seat, waiting for the doors to be slammed closed.

Chapter 22

What the hell was that buzzing noise?

Susannah wished whoever was conducting a conversation in the corner of her bedroom would shut the hell up. She tried to say so, but her tongue seemed to be sandpaper, glued to the bottom of her mouth. The voices faded. Quiet again.

She was on her back for some reason. She didn't sleep on her back. Was there something in her mouth?

The buzzing noise was back. It went black again.

Susannah's eye opened, but not because she meant it to. Someone had their fingers on her face, and then there was a bright light.

"Excuse me?" Well, that was what she tried to say. There was definitely something pressed against her tongue. That wasn't right. She started to struggle, and then all the agitated voices came back.

"Susannah? Can you hear me, love?"

She opened both eyes then. The lighting was horrible and, as she focused, she could see a strip light overhead. Maybe that was the source of the buzzing noise. Then a strange face came into view. Friendly, smiling, like she wanted Susannah to do well on her test.

"Nice of you to join us, Susannah. I'm Dr Gray. We've been a bit worried about you. Now, we had a breathing tube in just to make sure you were okay, but that can come out now if you give me a second."

The next few seconds made Susannah wish she'd stayed asleep.

There was a lot of handling her then, propping her up with pillows, and listening to her breathing with a stethoscope.

"All good," the doctor said, giving her and a nurse a brisk nod before leaving.

"What's happened?" Susannah's voice came out sounding like Kathleen Turner with a chest infection. "Wait, all I remember is smoke, but I couldn't wake up properly."

"You've had a lucky escape," the nurse said, patting Susannah's hand where an IV had been inserted and taped in place. "But there's a young lady out there bursting to see you, so I'll let her fill you in on the details."

"Tess?" Susannah tried to ask, but it came out as more of a croak. Nonetheless, the very person she most wanted to see came charging into the hospital room a minute later. Despite her private room, the door had been left ajar.

"Are you okay?"

Tess looked pretty roughed up. Her face was sooty, her eyes were red, and her hair was out of that permanent ponytail and hanging limply around her face. She had her arm in a sling and her clothes looked filthy. As she got closer, Susannah became aware of the smoky smell coming from her own body. It was nothing compared to the freshly extinguished barbecue scent that Tess brought in with her like a dust cloud.

Not that it stopped Susannah from grabbing that soot-streaked pyjama shirt and carefully pulling Tess close enough to kiss. "The pub?" Susannah asked.

Tess shook her head.

"Please tell me nobody was..." She couldn't say it. The thought of being responsible for anyone dying was too much.

"No, you were the only one there. Babs was away, and the Andersen boys were all safe at home."

Tess did her own inspection of Susannah, checking for injuries and who knew what else.

Susannah squirmed under the attention. "Unless I've suddenly turned into a pit bull, you can leave that to the human doctors."

"Are you saying I'm not human?" Tess smiled for the first time since coming in. That cheeky grin of hers was an instant painkiller.

Susannah sat up a bit straighter. "Ha-ha. How did you get so messy? It can't have spread all the way back to the houses, surely? Is Waffles okay?"

"He's fine. He's outside with Margo and Adam. The fire spooked him a little, but it didn't come near the house, thank God."

"Then how… Tess…did you—?"

"Do you want something to drink? I can ask the nurses if you're allowed anything more than the few sips of water you had when they took the tube out."

"Tess Robinson. Did you run into a burning building—into an actual fire—just to save me?" Susannah stared at Tess in something like amazement, the rest of her words deserting her. That kind of bravery was awe-inspiring and terrifying in turn. When had Susannah become someone worth risking that kind of danger for?

Even under the soot and the faint burn mark on her left cheek, the blush on Tess was obvious. "It was instinct! Nobody else knew you were there, and the fire engines took way too long. I had to, and I'd do it again, so don't even think about getting mad at me!"

"Mad at you?" Susannah got a good handful of the pyjamas that time. "I could kiss you!"

"Oh. Well, you can definitely do that."

So she did. They both did, for a few breathless moments. Very breathless, since neither of them had fully recovered.

"They'll want to check on you more." Tess pulled a chair to the side of the bed and took Susannah's hand in her good one. "And you probably have more questions, but can we just be like this for a moment? Just…be glad we're both still here?"

"Of course," Susannah said. "We'll take all the time you need."

A parade of doctors, nurses, and orderlies took up most of the next few hours. Susannah was wheeled around in a chair after her attempts to walk under her own steam ended quickly and with a lot of coughing.

"I'm not carrying you again," Tess warned. "I've got a potentially broken collarbone, so you'll have to listen to medical advice and take the wheels."

The hospital wasn't a major crisis centre, but it was the biggest facility in the area. Susannah took their reassuring words that she was fine to heart, and despite the pain levels and general exhaustion, she vowed not to wallow in the bad luck of it all. At least she was here to tell the tale.

They were back in her room when Tess brought it up, having choked down some vending machine coffee and half of the vanilla yoghurt that came with Susannah's otherwise untouched breakfast.

"The fire had already started when I woke up," Tess said. "I think it woke me, actually. I didn't see anyone around. But it's been bugging me, and I'm sure the police will be here at some point. Maybe some kind of fire investigator too? Anyway, they're going to at least suspect this might have been done deliberately." Tess was ticking things off on her fingers; clearly she had been working at some kind of theory.

But a theory about what? Surely she couldn't mean...

"I know this is probably me seeing one too many crime shows, but didn't Robin threaten the pub just last week? She said she'd take it from you, but there was no chance she could claim it as being your husband's. You said he put everything for it in your name."

Susannah felt a little too hazy for a business chat, but she tried to focus.

"I'm not saying she was sitting in the bushes with a can of petrol and some matches," Tess continued, "but anyone with her connections and a bit of money could find a willing wee bastard to do their dirty work."

"No, no. Absolutely not." Susannah prodded at the banana that sat by her plate. It looked like it wouldn't be ripe for a week yet. "Especially not since I saw her at the town hall yesterday. She heard me say that I was going to stay at the pub. Even if she'd had some dastardly scheme, she would have called it off if she knew there would be someone there to get hurt. Robin wants my money and the land; she isn't a murderer..."

"Susannah?"

They both looked up to see a stricken Robin Karlson in the doorway.

"What do you want?" Tess practically growled, gripping Susannah's blanket and clearly ready to fly into battle. "Only, I think the police probably want a word with you first."

"They do. I mean, I spoke to them." Robin hesitated for a moment before proceeding a few steps into the room. She had her hands clasped in front of her. Instead of her usual country tweeds, she seemed to have dressed in old riding gear, barely one step up from pyjamas. Her eyes were red-rimmed with none of her usual gaudy make-up in evidence. "Susannah, this isn't easy for me, so please do hear me out. I've come to apologise."

Susannah snorted in disbelief. "Come to do what?"

"It seems, uh, my young assistant, Jonathan... Apparently he's been having some strange ideas about how angry he thinks I am with you. I want you to know that although we've had our differences, I would never—*never, Susannah*—condone any such dangerous behaviour."

Susannah looked to Tess then back to Robin, stunned.

"You mean Jonathan set the fire?" Susannah asked. "Deliberately? Where is he now?"

"The police have him." Robin crossed the rest of the space to stand closer to Susannah's bed. She reached out as though she might take Susannah's hand for a moment, before diverting to pat aimlessly at the blanket. "The moment I saw him come in, covered in soot... well, I had no choice. I was straight on the phone to the police. It seems he's been taking my business dispute with you very personally. If this pub fire hadn't worked, they believe Midsummer was his next target."

"He would have burnt down the *house*?" Susannah almost choked on the jolt of panic chased by fear.

Robin looked almost as shaken at the thought as she was. Whatever her motives had been, she definitely loved the old place.

"But how would that have helped you get what you want?" Susannah asked. "You'd have had to rebuild. Was this about how he felt about Jimmy? I don't understand."

"Very convenient," Tess spoke up. "Even if we take Jonathan out of the equation, that doesn't neutralise you. You could be back to harassing Susannah again by next week."

Robin sat on the edge of the bed, picking at her fingernails absently. "No, no. That's all done with. If anything worse had happened, if you had... I don't know how I could have lived with myself. It's bad enough that you two landed in hospital, but I see now I had latched on to the wrong details. I simply missed my brother and wanted to honour his memory. I should have been more careful about what I said around Jonathan. I knew he had a certain...fixation on James, for years, and he resented you as a result. I didn't understand how deep the bitterness ran. My disagreement with you aggravated things, spurred him on to...this. Anyway, I'll raise no further dispute over Midsummer. It's yours, Susannah, however we got to here. I've already called off my solicitors."

"Really?" Susannah's voice was fading. She helped herself to an ice chip. "If this is some kind of ploy to make me let my guard down while I'm vulnerable, in hospital..."

"You have my word it's not," Robin replied, standing and offering her hand for Susannah to shake.

Susannah met her gaze, sure and steady, searching for any last signs of deception. She didn't take the outstretched hand.

Robin seemed to understand, withdrawing the gesture. Too much, too soon for all the months of bad blood. Even so, the sincere expression on her face didn't waver for a second. "I do so wish it hadn't taken something this awful for me to finally see my grief with some perspective. If I can do anything to make this up to you, I insist you tell me at your first convenience. I just wanted to tell you in person. I'll go." She turned.

"Robin?" Susannah called after her.

"Yes?"

"I know we've both exchanged angry words, but there's something that I haven't been able to shake since you said it, and—"

"About James? Resenting you for the marriage?" Robin asked with a sigh. "I knew I'd hurt you with that one. I did feel bad even then, believe it or not. But I'm afraid my source on what James said was our unreliable former employee, so I think you can stop worrying about it."

Relief coursed through Susannah. It was just Jonathan and his bitter fantasies. She should have known.

"I should go, let you rest," Robin finished. True to her word, she turned on her heel and marched out.

Susannah didn't know what to do with herself. Was the nightmare really over? Robin certainly seemed to think so.

Tess watched Robin go with a scowl. "She's lucky I didn't kick her ass right out of here for everything she's put you through. All very well to be sorry in hindsight, but look what her hate and nonsense stirred up!"

"You keep that temper, Dr Robinson," Susannah warned, although she was as touched by Tess and her protective streak as she was devastated that Jonathan could be so whipped up by Robin's ranting that he would commit this heinous crime.

"You could have died." Tess's voice trembled. She squeezed Susannah's hand a little too tightly. "We both could have."

"Oh come on. This isn't prime-time television. The queer women survived! Let's not be all doom and gloom about this."

"Lady Karlson?" A policeman stood at the door. He looked about nineteen. "We'd like to ask you some questions. We have someone in custody over the fire."

Susannah suppressed a weary sigh.

He eased his way in, the hi-vis vest covered by bits of equipment, a shiny black truncheon hanging from his hip. His female partner followed suit. "If you're feeling up to it, we'd like to have a word about events surrounding the fire at The Spiky Thistle?"

"Yes, yes. Come in and let's get it over with. Can Tess stay? She's my…"

"Girlfriend," Tess supplied. "I'm the one who got her out of the fire, so it'll save you time to talk to us both."

"Oh, so you're the hero!" The female officer said, losing her cool expression for a moment. "I hope you know there are a ton of reporters dying to talk to you. It's like a rugby scrum outside the hospital, and all they want to know about is you, saving the lady of the manor no less!"

Tess sputtered at the information.

Susannah took her hand. "I don't think we're ready for the press. Thanks for letting us know, though. And Tess here really is a big damn hero." The sweet blush rose on Tess's cheeks again, so Susannah risked a coughing fit to lean in and kiss her cheek.

"Very good," the first police officer said, pulling out his notebook. "Now let's start with where you were earlier in the evening."

Susannah scanned the pick-up area by the hospital's quiet private entrance for Tess in her much-maligned car. She hoped Tess had been able to run the gauntlet of reporters without getting stopped. Since the X-rays revealed her lover's collarbone was just bruised, Tess had been allowed to drive.

Relief flooded through Susannah as Tess drove into view. She was bundling herself into the passenger seat less than two minutes later.

In the back of the car, Waffles greeted her from the safety of his crate.

"So, *girlfriend*, huh?" Susannah said. "And a nationally famous hero, no less."

Tess didn't blush this time, just winked and blew a kiss at Susannah while navigating the byzantine route to get out of hospital grounds.

"Well, we needed a word for us," Tess said. "And since I plan on dating you a whole bunch more than we've managed so far, I thought 'girlfriend' just about covered it. Do you have any objections?"

"None whatsoever. We'll hear from the police tomorrow about the investigation, but they're pretty sure they've got their man. All the evidence seems to corroborate it."

"Did you tell them about Robin? Was she really not involved?"

"Police raided Jonathan's home, seized a bunch of plans, and have confirmed she was clueless about his darker activities," Susannah answered. "She was definitely picking fights with me, but he was escalating it without her knowledge. Not big on details, my dear sister-in-law."

"How are you feeling? Are you sure they should have let you out this soon?"

"I'm fine. If I get dizzy or breathless, I should go back in, but you really did save my life. Did I thank you for that yet?"

Tess braked for a red light ahead, making a show of thinking about it. "You know, I don't think you have? Sure, you were unconscious, but you have a PA. Would a card and some flowers have killed you?" She snorted with laughter at herself.

Susannah leaned in for a kiss rather than roll her eyes. "Thank you."

"Ow." Tess said when they parted, cars behind them honking because the light had turned green. "That bruising isn't fun."

"Sorry." Susannah fought a surge of guilt. "I couldn't resist. Still, you should rest."

"No delivering calves for me today, that's for sure. Adam will have to stand in for me."

"Well, I happen to know somewhere very comfortable you could relax tonight. Far away from a crime scene and the smell of burnt wood," Susannah said. "My bed is definitely big enough for two."

Waffles barked.

"Okay, three, but he has to stay at the bottom."

"Good luck with that," Tess replied, driving them towards Midsummer, trying to hold back a beaming smile as she went.

Chapter 23

Tess held her mug of tea and stood by the front door of the vet surgery, trying to watch the events out in front of the pub without being too obvious. Clearly, she hadn't succeeded, as in less than a minute, Joan crossed the street from the café to come and get a better view beside Tess.

"What are they saying to Susannah?" Joan asked.

Tess shrugged. She was neither a lip reader nor a psychic.

"I mean, what did they say to her before this?"

"How would I know?" Tess tried to look innocent.

Joan's answer was a reproachful look.

Great. Seemed the whole village knew where Tess had been spending most nights since the fire.

They continued to watch from a distance as Susannah talked with the fire officer and a senior-looking police officer. There was lots of pointing and gesturing, but it was impossible to tell if the news was just bad or downright terrible.

"Have they settled on what caused the fire?" Babs asked, approaching from the opposite direction. "Susannah can't start rebuilding until that's all settled."

"The initial finding was arson, so I imagine this is their final report," Tess replied, bracing herself for hostilities. "There should be an insurance agent somewhere about as well. It's a lot of stress for her."

"They want to take a look at Robin Karlson," Joan said.

"They should," Babs agreed. "And none of us has trusted Jonathan since he went to the dark side."

Tess almost choked on her tea. Babs and Joan were actually acknowledging one another.

"Of course, I'm being paid regardless, but I can't stand being idle," Babs concluded.

"I'm surprised you haven't started rebuilding it yourself." Joan gestured towards the burnt-out building.

It was just small talk, really, but Tess could hear the rustiness in it.

"Give me time," Babs replied. When she finally looked at Joan, her gaze was so soft. "And thanks, by the way, for giving me a place to put my head down. I was offered rooms on the estate, of course, but I didn't want to be in the way."

Tess could feel the pointed look from Joan coming her way. "Listen," she cut it off, "there's plenty of room, and it wouldn't be disturbing our sleepovers to have you stay over. What's gotten into you two? I've been warned since I got here that you're the Montague and Capulet of Hayleith, and now you're staying over at Joan's?" If they could stick their noses into Tess's business, she could damn well do the same in return.

"It's possible..." Joan began, dragging out the words and letting a hint of her usually imperceptible Jamaican twang wrap around the vowels, "... that the fire was a bit of a wake-up call."

"You should have seen this one." Babs sounded more than a little smug as she waved at Joan. "Well, I wasn't here, but I've been told she was crying like a right sap when she thought I'd been in there. I notice she didn't charge in, though, playing the hero like some fool we know."

"With this hip?" Joan scoffed. She turned to Tess. "Anyway, it was impressive what you did for Susannah. And as you probably know now, if someone is worth running into a burning building for, then you don't let them go."

"But you didn't—" Babs started to interrupt.

"I would have, if I hadn't been told you were away. I only cried because I knew you were safe. So that's how much you know, woman."

Tess smiled at the fondness between them as they argued. "I've always meant to ask, and I might not get another chance, with the way you bicker," she said. "What was the big fight all about? You haven't spoken to each other in years, right?"

Babs and Joan exchanged a look, one of those silent discussions that couples had.

"It was just one of those things," Babs said, patting Joan's upper arm. "Water under the bridge."

"No, that's not fair to you," Joan said. She turned to Tess. "I was scared. Babs gave up just about everything to be with me, and I was so bothered by what people thought that I ran away. Only I didn't get very far."

"You went from working at the pub together to running the café across the road?" Tess asked.

"Lord Karlson had just bought us out—bought the pub for Susannah," Babs explained. "I said if she didn't want people knowing we were more than colleagues, if she was that ashamed of me, well, she could take her half and go."

"It was all a bit nasty for a while," Joan said. "So we gradually stopped speaking. I hated how much it hurt each time, and that was just easier. I suppose we never stopped caring."

Babs took her hand and dropped a smacker of a kiss on Joan's cheek. It left behind an imprint of bright pink lipstick.

Joan was slow to wipe it away.

"Heads up," Babs said at the sight of Susannah walking away from the officials outside the pub. "We'll expect an update later, Doc."

"But—"

"Bye!" Joan and Babs said in chorus, heading off to the café.

"Here you go." Tess set down a mug of black coffee for Susannah on the table in the vets' staffroom. Margo and Adam had been banished to the treatment rooms. She didn't care whether or not they had appointments. "What did the investigators say?"

"Pretty much what we expected. Fire started deliberately, no CCTV. They did find some kind of petrol can with a partial fingerprint though, which confirms it was Jonathan once and for all."

"Isn't that a bit sloppy?"

"I thought so. Apparently he's been nursing a huge grudge ever since Jimmy broke up with him. Jonathan always blamed me. I do feel better knowing he's locked up."

"Me too. When can you start work on rebuilding?"

"A while yet." Susannah paused. "Did I see you speaking to Joan before?"

Tess nodded.

"I'm going to ask her about getting a temporary liquor licence at the café for the evenings. People around here need a place to let off steam after a hard day's work. I'm not worried about the lost business, but I am worried about the effects it could have."

Tess reached across the table and grabbed Susannah's hand, rubbing her thumb across the knuckles. "You're not responsible for the whole village, you know."

"Yes, but still—"

"Not to mention you got the go-ahead for your development of the estate. You might even have your sister-in-law over your shoulder at some point, offering 'helpful' suggestions."

"I'm beginning to think you have a vindictive streak, Tess. But we are ready, and the building work starts next week. Robin, though, she's really coming around. Guilt is a great leveller."

"Did I mention it's hot when you're all Businesswoman of the Year?"

There was a commotion outside the door, and Tess glanced towards the noise.

"Sounds a bit rowdy for a neutered Alsatian," Susannah remarked just as the door banged open.

"Tessie! There you are!"

Tess almost knocked her half-empty mug across the table as she jumped to her feet. "Caroline?"

"Can you tell these friends of yours that I do know how to behave in a veterinary surgery?"

Adam and Margo were doing a fine job of trying to hold her back, but sheer entitlement seemed to have her overpowering them. Caroline always did have a strong "I want to see the manager" energy about her, with the haircut to match.

"It's okay, guys. Caroline, what are you doing here?"

"Well, don't just stand there, hero of the hour, give me a hug!" Caroline swooped in, but Tess ducked her open arms.

"No thanks." The floral scent of her perfume was more cloying than Tess remembered.

"Oh, one of your moods, is it? Well, I was just on my way to Edinburgh for a little thing called my hen weekend. We get all the way to Berwick, and the trains just stop…total chaos. The girls decided to wait it out, but when I saw how close you were…one hire car later and here I am! Thought I should make sure you're still coping, now that you've taken up running into burning buildings of all the things."

"She is coping!" Margo replied.

Tess waved her off. "Why would you think I wouldn't be coping? It's been more than a year since we split, and as you can see, I've got a lovely little practice."

"Oh, Tessie, you know what I mean. You were trying to tell me you'd already met someone, and when I spoke to Barb—"

"Babs," Tess corrected.

"Babs, yes. Well, she wasn't entirely convincing. So I thought, why not round you up and drag you to this hen night, really help you get over me once and for all?"

They all seemed stunned into silence.

"Uh…" Tess was fumbling for how many different ways to say no.

Caroline was off and running again, smoothing down the blazer she was wearing over one of her endless supply of blue-and-white striped tops, complete with the mandatory skinny jeans and heels. "Don't believe we've met." She gave Susannah a haughty once-over. "You're a bit overdressed for a vet nurse, aren't you? Oh, you weren't in court, were you?"

Other people might have been thrown by the hurricane of Caroline's conversation, but Susannah took it entirely in stride. Not bothering to stand, she made a point of inspecting her manicure. "Not this week, no. Caroline, was it?"

"That's right! Dr Caroline Goddard, but I'm sure it's all very informal around here."

"Quite the contrary," Susannah replied, and it was almost a drawl. She sounded every bit the bored country lady. "Titles really should be adhered to, don't you agree?"

"Well, yes, yes I do!"

Tess had to hide her mouth behind her hand. Susannah had read Caroline for exactly the snob that she was.

"Then it's a pleasure to meet you, Dr Goddard. I'm Lady Karlson, and these wonderful vets here look after all the equine care on my estate."

Caroline lit up like she'd finally found her people. "Well, at my practice we take our important clients out to lunch, but I suppose coffee in the staff room is another way to go. I don't suppose you're in the mood for a little jolly in Edinburgh? The girls would just love that." She waved out the window at a compact, mud-flecked rental car parked outside as if ready to whisk them away that minute.

"Great offer." Susannah finally unfolded her long frame from the chair. She took the necessary couple of steps to be at Tess's side. "But we have plans this weekend. Not terribly outdoorsy ones, if you catch my drift. Although there's always the hot tub."

Caroline looked between them as Susannah slipped her arm around Tess's waist, letting it settle there like it belonged.

Gathering herself, Tess put her hand on top of Susannah's at her waist and gave her ex a beaming smile.

"This…this is Susan?"

"Susannah," Tess replied. "Lady Susannah Karlson. Don't let us keep you. It's quite a drive up to the city."

"Especially in some dreadful little rental car," Susannah said, her polite laugh tinkling and very fake. "They'll give you any old thing. Unless you have someone like Tess here—she has wonderful taste in cars."

Margo was making faces at Tess, who couldn't let herself look properly, in case she burst out laughing.

"Does she now? Still, good to see you're doing well for yourself, Tessie."

"She prefers Tess," Susannah answered for her. "Or is that just from me, darling?" She fitted about six *A*'s, twelve *H*'s and half of the Elgin marbles into the extra-hoity-toity way she said *darling*.

Tess could have kissed her for it. So she did. Great little habit that was becoming.

"Right, better be going," Caroline said like it was all her idea. "Do let me know about your wedding RSVP; the date's not so far off now."

Then she was gone, leaving them all to collectively lose it as soon as the door closed behind her.

Adam got hold of himself first. "Oh, that showed her. Good on you, Lady K."

"I think someone was after a one-night stand en route to the hen night," Margo said.

Susannah nodded. "Definitely. She thought Tess'd be just waiting to fall back into her arms. Well, we showed her you're definitely off the market, didn't we?"

"I am?"

"Yes."

"Then we did," Tess replied, glowing from confirmation of what she was already pretty sure about. "And can you stop looking so scandalized, Adam? Did you really think we've been playing Monopoly all the time we've been spending together?"

"And it won't, uh, affect our contract?" he asked, which Tess had to concede was a fair question.

"Absolutely not," Susannah replied. "And if for some reason Tess never wants to see me again, you can simply swap in another vet to deal with my horses. Speaking of which, I have two fine boys being delivered today. I had to delay their arrival with all that's been happening. Tess?"

Tess reached for her jacket and vet bag. "Did you think up new names for them?"

Susannah groaned.

"What?" Tess asked.

"It's just that ever since you suggested Andy and Jamie, well...they've kind of stuck in my head."

"Andy and Jamie?" Margo repeated. "Why is that a problem? Not the fanciest names, but still."

"I've been trying to avoid more tennis names, to change up the habit at my stables. But here we are with the Murray brothers joining the ranks."

"It suits them," Tess said. "Come on, let's get up there and help them settle in."

Chapter 24

TODAY WAS THE DAY. THE big day. Maybe the biggest of all the days so far.

Susannah couldn't help wishing Tess was already at her side, but she would be seeing her soon enough. That was what mattered. Now it was just down to the last few details.

Nails? Immaculately manicured. Hair? Styled and set. Dress? Sitting perfectly, thanks to that wonderful tailor in Glasgow. The speech? On index cards, if the nerves really grabbed hold. Otherwise it was all filed away in Susannah's memory, along with a hundred other details that she could let go of once the day was over and done with. Wouldn't that be a relief?

"Tess just arrived," Finn said, popping their head around the door. Stylish to a fault, they had really pushed the boat out with a crimson waistcoat that matched the floral arrangements that dotted the hall and seating area. "Do you want me to sneak her back here for a quick morale boost or just show her to her seat?"

"Let her go and sit down," Susannah said, although a hit of Tess's calming presence was tempting. "The music is cued?"

"Just hit the button on your phone and wait ten seconds before walking in," Finn said. "You'll knock 'em dead out there, Boss. This has been a long time coming, eh?"

"Couldn't have done it without you. Tell that hunky partner of yours we'll all be wanting a dance with him later."

"If I tell him now, he'll go into hiding," Finn replied. "But I'll make sure he sticks around to show off his two left feet. See you out there!"

Then Susannah was alone again in the small room leading into Midsummer's *de facto* ballroom. It was supposed to be a dining room, really, but Susannah rarely had a chance to fill it. The last event before today had been when the councillors had told her they were following Robin's advice not to back Susannah and her plans.

But thanks to Tess being her charming and delightful self, those same councillors had voted yes anyway. Now Susannah was well on her way to transforming Midsummer into the place she had always wanted it to be. It certainly hadn't seemed possible even a few months ago.

Susannah cued up the music on her phone and waited the requisite ten seconds. Then the door was open, and she was striding across the floor to the designated spot. Every head in the room turned to stare at her. There was only one face she was looking for, though.

And there she was, right in front. Tess led the round of applause as if she were watching a triple-bill of Beyoncé, Madonna, and Lady Gaga, but the enthusiasm in the room quickly matched hers. Most importantly, she looked stunning in her navy-blue suit and pale pink shirt, with her hair down to mark the special occasion.

Susannah reached the glass podium and raised her hands to quiet the crowd. She would never quite get used to this part of it. "Thank you all for being here today. If you could take your seats, I just have a few words I wanted to share with you."

Just over a hundred people did exactly that, and the room hushed in anticipation.

Susannah swallowed to combat her dry throat. "A lot of people didn't think this day would come," she began, and she felt Robin's eyes on her from the back of the room. She looked up, and their eyes met. A nod came from Robin, confirming that their truce held, that all was well. "There have been a lot of days where I was one of those doubters. But after years of planning and months of hard, hard work, we're finally here."

Another ripple of applause broke out.

"And while there's much still to be done, we can declare Phase One complete. So welcome, all of you, to a new age here at Midsummer. The Midsummer Animal Sanctuary is now officially open!"

Tess was on her feet. Robin clapped as loudly as anyone. This time the applause around the room was loud and confident, helped by all the new staff who looked pleased to be there. Next week the pub would reopen too, which might be the biggest highlight of all for the people of Hayleith.

Babs and Joan were sitting together. That was still nothing short of a miracle, and one Susannah was grateful for.

"So, please, help yourself to drinks, and have some food from our fabulous chef. I expect to see you all on the dance floor before the night is out!"

Relieved to be done with the speaking part, Susannah accepted the ridiculous giant scissors from Finn and cut the purple velvet ribbon that hung across the doorframe behind her. She acknowledged yet more clapping, but the moment it was done, she strode across to reunite with Tess.

"Hey, you," Susannah said, melting into one of their easy embraces. "I wasn't sure you were going to make it."

"It was touch and go, but she finally delivered about two hours ago."

People came by offering handshakes and congratulations before Susannah and Tess could keep talking. Susannah accepted them graciously. The one-on-one parts were slightly easier, though not by much. It was a little less awful with Tess by her side. "Usually when you're gone all night because someone's giving birth, you come home and tell me about a calf called Daffodil," Susannah said. "Tell me Margo and Adam haven't been as adventurous with the baby names?"

"Sticking with Baby Boy Elliot for now. There's been some heated debate, though," Tess replied, accepting two glasses of bubbly from a passing server and giving one to Susannah. "I believe Margo said that if Adam wanted to name their son after him, he'd have to… Well, it was something about a bowling ball and his nostril but with a lot more swear words."

"Ah. Shall I send something over to the hospital?"

"She'll be home tonight. But I already picked out some things. From, uh, from us both?"

Susannah smiled as she claimed another quick kiss. "I like that. Another level of official. Despite how chaotic it's been, you're still not running. From this, or us."

"Never been much of a runner," Tess replied. "Not when everything good is right here. Great job, great woman, my best friends, nice house… what should I run from exactly?"

"You make a good point. I'm going to have to make the rounds for a little while. Think you can spare me?"

"Only if you come back every so often," Tess said. "I am a frequent guest at Midsummer, you know, and I expect a certain level of VIP treatment."

"I think that can be arranged." For a moment, as she held Tess's hand, Susannah considered blowing off the party and sneaking upstairs. Unfortunately, being the centre of attention made sneaking anywhere almost impossible. "And I want to see you on that floor at some point. The world deserves to see your step-perfect *Mamma Mia* choreography, Tess."

"That was one time!" Tess called after her.

Susannah was already off and wending her way through the crowd. Midsummer didn't feel empty anymore. Her step faltered for a second, and she considered the house around her. Within a moment or two, her gaze drifted back to Tess.

The house may not have felt empty anymore, but most of all, it finally felt like a home.

Other Books from Ylva Publishing

www.ylva-publishing.com

Major Surgery

Lola Keeley

ISBN: 978-3-96324-145-1
Length: 198 pages (69,000 words)

Surgeon and department head Veronica has life perfectly ordered...until the arrival of a new Head of Trauma. Cassie is a brash ex-army surgeon, all action and sharp edges, not interested in rules or playing nice with icy Veronica. However when they're forced to work together to uncover a scandal, things get a little heated in surprising ways.

A lesbian romance about cutting to the heart of matters.

Up on the Roof

A.L. Brooks

ISBN: 978-3-95533-988-3
Length: 245 pages (88,000 words)

When a storm wreaks havoc on bookish Lena's well-ordered world, her laid-back new neighbor, Megan, offers her a room. The trouble is they've been clashing since the day they met. How can they now live under the same roof? Making it worse is the inexplicable pull between them that seems hard to resist. A fun, awkward, and sweet British romance about the power of opposites attracting.

You're Fired
Shaya Crabtree

ISBN: 978-3-95533-754-4
Length: 193 pages (61,000 words)

When poor college student Rose Walsh gives out an inappropriate gag gift at her office Christmas party, it backfires horribly. The gift's recipient is her boss, the esteemed president of Gio Corp., Vivian Tracey, and the only thing that can save Rose now is her smarts.

Instead of firing her, Vivian blackmails math major Rose into joining her on a business trip to New York to investigate an embezzlement. A week out of state with a woman she can barely stand seems like the last thing Rose wants to do with her winter vacation. Only, maybe Vivian is not as bad as she seems. Maybe they can even become friends...or more.

Changing the Script
Lee Winter

ISBN: 978-3-96324-296-0
Length: 317 pages (104,000 words)

LA-based indie filmmaker Alex Levitin finds herself in New Zealand to save the "worst movie ever". Things might go easier if she didn't almost run over the standoffish local cop, Sam Keegan, and if the film wasn't being sabotaged. As Alex and Sam reluctantly join forces to find the set saboteur, attraction flares.

A funny, small-town lesbian romance about clashing cultures and daring to dream.

About Lola Keeley

Lola Keeley is a writer and coder. After moving to London to pursue her love of theatre, she later wound up living every five-year-old's dream of being a train driver on the London Underground. She has since emerged, blinking into the sunlight, to find herself writing books. She now lives in Edinburgh, Scotland, with her wife and four cats.

CONNECT WITH LOLA

Website: www.lolakeeley.co.uk

Facebook: www.facebook.com/lolakeeley

E-Mail: divalola@gmail.com

A Roll in the Hay

ISBN: 978-3-96324-355-4

Also available as e-book.

Published by Ylva Publishing, legal entity of Ylva Verlag, e.Kfr.

Ylva Verlag, e.Kfr.
Owner: Astrid Ohletz
Am Kirschgarten 2
65830 Kriftel
Germany

www.ylva-publishing.com

First edition: 2020

Credits
Edited by Lee Winter and Michelle Aguilar
Cover Design by Caroline Manchoulas
Print Layout by Streetlight Graphics

Printed in Great Britain
by Amazon

57190242R00118